DARK
HORIZON

N.M. BLACK

PLAYLIST

Happy Death Day- Alien Ant Farm
My Own Summer- Deftones
Hoodie- Hey Violet
Everything Goes Black- Skillet
It's Alright- Mother Mother
Hey, Ma- Bon Iver
Like a Nightmare- Never Say Die
Power Over Me- Dermot Kennedy
The Funeral- Band of Horses
Cringe- Matt Maeson
Never Stop- Hidden Citizens
Hold My Girl (acoustic version)- Geroge Ezra
Leave It All Behind- Sleeping With Sirens
Medicine- USS
Rise Above It- I Prevail, Justin Stone
I Remember Way Too Much- Mod Sun
Not Too Late- Moon Taxi
Hold You Down- X Ambassadors
Bruises- Lewis Capaldi
Walk- Pantera

Superbeast- Rob Zombie
Adrenalize- In This Moment
Till I Found You- Phil Wickham
Fire Up The Night- New Medicine

Listen to the playlist here: https://open.spotify.com/
playlist/7wXWovjzGVybqGY50neCX9?
si=stGzzXgWQDutgfi6xb8NEQ

ZOMBIE BREEDS

Gen One zombies- They're "normal" for all intents and purposes with no special abilities. Their eyes a bright yellow, pale skin coloring. Easy to kill."

Sprinters- They're incredibly fast, not smart and very weak. It doesn't take much to overpower them. A single shot kill is achievable.

Tanks- Slow but strong. Picture that giant from the shower scene in Resident Evil. The only way to kill them is to sever their heads from their spine. A bullet will not stop them.

Pukers or Boilers- Exactly how they sound, vomits on attacker, quickly infects if gotten into eyes, mouth, nose, or open wounds. Not as easy to kill unless you have long range weapons. Distance is key.

Addicts and Crazies- their narcotic of choice or their mental diagnosis, will determine their *special abilities*.

Some have bursts of energy, others are very slow. Some can even jump and scale objects and buildings. Their most pronounced feature is the bright red rim around their irises and their veins are highly visible. Never count them as a one shot kill, and always keep your distance. They are highly unpredictable.

Demon Z's- They're smaller than Gen One zombies, thin and pale, with fully blacked out eyes. Rather than the typical grunts zombies make, they have a banshee-like screech that can debilitate anyone or anything in close range. They're also extremely fast which makes them hard to kill. Another clear trait of a Demon is the black tar they constantly spew.

Hybrid- No longer human, but not undead either. Can still die like a human though.

*Cidiots- City Idiot (Urban Dictionary Definition; The person who dwells in a city but **ventures** into **rural** areas to perform acts of **stupidity**. A classic cidiot cannot read a map, is terrified of "rednecks" (anyone the cidiot perceived to be rural is a redneck) and cannot take directions.

PROLOGUE

Lucie

February 17th, one year ago....

It's been three days since the outbreak started, the warning alarm still ringing out across the city, eliciting chaos and panic from those still trying to make their escape. People line the streets, trying desperately to outrun the virus that continues to spread out of control. Vehicles crammed bumper to bumper as they try to evade the ever-growing population of zombies, but getting nowhere fast. Families separated trying to survive in smaller numbers, but nothing changes the outcome of their fate.

I've thrived on these streets for years, and know every back alley, detour and unused road in this city, making it easy for me to navigate without drawing attention to myself and skating under the military's radar. This is just like any other day for me, fighting for survival, but these Cidiots, they don't stand a chance. Their life of convenience is no more. Those they feared, those whose life has been a constant struggle, are going to be the ones that survive.

I don't have much, being practically homeless, the sum of my life is in two duffle bags in the back, making my getaway that much easier. Especially now, since I'm down a person. We agreed that if we didn't meet up at our designated spot by a certain time, the other is to leave. No questions asked. But I can't ignore the nagging feeling that I should see if Bea is alive. As much as I don't think so, that old bird is feisty as shit, and she might actually bite one of them back.

She's in her 70's and can wield a baseball bat like a major league player, with the mouth of a sailor. I made the mistake of breaking into her house one night, thinking no one was home, but boy was I wrong. I climbed through her living room window and before my feet touched the carpet, she had me on my ass gasping for the breath she knocked out of me. That woman had stripped me of my homemade bat, knocked me half unconscious and poured herself a drink before I even saw her from the shadows. The next night was the first of many that I ate dinner with Bea.

Fuck!

I yanked the wheel of the stolen SUV to the left and head down a side street and through someone's backyard, dodging a small group of z's that have currently made a buffet of someone's family dog. I couldn't live with myself if she was still alive and I left her to a similar fate.

I pull around to the side door of her house and check

that there's no z's, before jumping out to go in after her. Fuck, I hope she's here.

As I approach the screen door, my worst fear is playing out right in front of me. There, pinned up against the counter is Bea, and one of them has her caged and lurches at her repeatedly. She must be in shock because she just stands there, arms stretched out in front of her, frozen in place, barely dodging the zombies' constant attack.

I don't hesitate, grabbing my own version of Neagan's Lucille, as I fling open the screen door, catching its attention. Its head practically does a 180 as it takes in fresh meat and I can't stop the curse that leaves my lips. Joe, her brother and best friend, stares back at me through those yellow infected eyes, but I know that's no longer him. The virus controls him now.

He steps away from Bea, and I now have his full attention and I plan to keep it that way until she can get out the door to my "borrowed" vehicle. I glance towards her to try and telepathically relay this and to make sure she's ok, but she won't make eye contact with me to confirm. If I can keep Joe from turning around, she can make it to the truck and we can make a break for it. But she still hasn't moved a muscle.

"Bea!" I shout, trying to catch her attention and snap her into gear, but all that manages to do is solidify the unwanted advance of zombie Joe.

I step to the side, wanting to put the counter between us, but he surprises me and leaps up, clearing the counter completely, as agile as an Olympic athlete. We crash to the floor as our limbs tangle, each of us fighting for the upper hand and he knocks my bat from my grasp. I thrash my head back and forth trying to keep his snapping jaw from making contact, but it's no use. He's stronger and much more determined.

Just as I let my arms go limp and accept my fate, Joe's eyes go wide in fear and he freezes in place. Slowly, his body slumps to the side, crashing down to the floor beside me, as my heart continues to race at how close I came to joining team Z.

And there where he stood, with a large kitchen knife suspended from her hand dripping with black ichor, stands Bea.

CHAPTER 1

Lucie

"**W**oman! Get in this truck before I leave you here for dead!" I shout out the window at Bea, who is ignoring the not so small group of zombies coming our way. Sure, the thick blankets of snow slow them down, but it slows us down too.

"Shut your mouth or I'll kick your emo ass!" she shouts back, drawing more unwelcome attention.

"It's steampunk, not emo. And if I die for this shit, you best believe I'm coming to find you and bite your ass!" I toss out, as my knee begins to bounce uncontrollably at the sight of the incoming hoard of teeth that are getting closer in my rearview mirror. I drop the plow into the fresh powder, ready to take off the second Bea gives me the signal.

She tosses the last of her personal haul into the truck and jumps in, slapping her hand on the dash to signal she's ready. I punch the gas, shooting us into our seats and take off before we're swarmed. My truck can handle plowing through them and the snow, but it's not fun cleaning out their guts and shit from the undercarriage. And don't even get me started on the smell.

"Listen, you don't hear me complain every time you put us in compromising positions for, *he who should not be named*." She throws at me with an eyebrow cocked and a wicked smirk stretched across her face. She's right. I've done many trips and side excursions that are not sanctioned and definitely not considered safe by any means, putting us in precarious situations, for the man in question.

He who should not be named is named that for a very good reason. Many arguments have ensued at just the use of Chris's name in this truck. Chris is both mine *and* Bea's kryptonite, but for very different reasons. Bea is completely repulsed by his existence and voices it- loudly, I might add- that she is disappointed he's survived the apocalypse, whenever given the chance. But for me, Chris is both my weakness and my strength. He has this ability to make me think I can do anything, be anything with him by my side, and at the same time, holds the power to break me apart.

Just the thought of him sends shivers of heat, both good and bad throughout my body. I can't help my reaction to him, trust me, I've tried. Right now, however, my anger is definitely winning out this time around and I do nothing to temper it.

When I left the other day, I was pissed at him for what happened the night before I left, and I still am. We always spend time together before I head out on scavenging trips, it's something we've done since the beginning. But that night was different. That night *he* was different.

Chris runs his finger along one of the straps that encase my left thigh and my breath catches in the back of my throat. He's never done this. Never been this close, this forward in his actions toward me. I've never allowed *anyone to touch me before, and I'm not sure what to do, but I won't stop him either.*

He doesn't say a word or look at anything other than where his finger meets the leather on my leg. I hold my breath as he slides it back and forth, loosening the strap with each pass and glides his hand beneath it, but never coming in actual contact with my body. As close as he always seems to get, he never actually *touches me directly. Always indirectly.*

"Why do you always wear this...stuff?" Chris gestures to the rest of my outfit. I have on a leather corset, with matching forearm guards. Leather straps cling to my thighs and shoulders, holstering a weapon on each side.

He always talks shit about my leathers, trying to get a rise out of me. And it works. Every damn time. He taunts me like an older sibling would taunt their younger, more annoying one.

But I don't want to be his sibling.

He can be relentless at times, having no idea what my life was truly like while growing up. Having no idea what it feels like to struggle with no family, no house and no money.

But this time it's different.

This time I'm not going to hold back to save his feelings or mine, no matter how long I've waited for this moment. For once, I want him to see how adult I can really be. How experienced I really am.

When I gather the nerve to look at him, I falter at the intensity in his eyes but regain my composure quickly before I deliver the truth that might end this before it even has the chance to begin.

"I grew up on the streets, fighting for every meal, every penny and every day to live. Crashing in parks, under bridges or from couch to couch, just to stay under the radar of child services. I had to learn to protect myself at a young age. Always play defence." His hand freezes its movements and I shrug as though it's no big deal. Because to me, it's not. Like I said, this was my life.

He slowly withdraws his hand and turns his body to face me and locks his gaze on mine. "That doesn't explain the wardrobe at all. And why were you running from child services? I thought they were supposed to help people, you know, in your situation." *His voice takes on a low growl and the last word comes out in disgust causing my anger to rise instantly, ready to defend myself for something out of my control.*

He looks away, clearly uncomfortable with my reaction to the topic and I'm not so sure he can handle my answer and what it implies. But I don't care that he's uncomfortable. I lived through uncomfortable. I embrace uncomfortable. He always sees me as this little girl, but right now, I am about to open his eyes and show him just how little I'm not. He's pushed too far and now he will understand exactly where my anger and distrust stem from.

And this time, I won't be giving him a dumbed-down version of my horror story, no, this time he will have to deal with the nightmares just like I do.

"Being placed in the system is usually worse than being homeless. Moved around from school to school if you don't fit in with your current family, having to adapt to home after home, and get along with complete strangers who want nothing to do with you. Most *times. At least if you're homeless, you don't have to worry about the ones meant to protect you demanding payment, in a form other than what is promised to them by the government. Or have your step-siblings that you're forced to share a room with try to force things on you, or to try and take one of the few things you possess of your own." I let the last of that sentence trail off, giving him the full effect of its meaning and letting it sink in. Let him picture the things I pray to never see again, to never dream about again, before I finish shattering the happy life bubble he was so lucky to have experienced while I starved more nights than I didn't.*

"The leather straps slow down those hands that get a little over affectionate with their new housemate, giving me time to get away or defend myself. They also protected me from people who didn't want me as a new house mate, and stopped knives, shivs and any other sharp object intending me harm from hitting vital organs or causing serious damage. And as of late, that includes teeth." His

head snaps back in my direction and his eyes narrow on me, as though he's angry at my last statement. Too bad. Time to open your eyes and see the real world around you. I'm not going to sugarcoat shit for him or anyone else anymore.

"You think this is me trying to look good? That I'm making some kind of fashion statement?" A maniacal laugh escapes my throat as I match his glare with one of my own. He thinks because I'm young that I haven't lived, or have no experience but in all actuality, I probably have more than he does.

"This is me trying to stay alive, trying to protect myself from the things that go bump in the night. You should know by now Chris, not all monsters hide under our beds."

The sound of Bea's laughter drags me from my thoughts as she assumes she's won the argument due to my silence, and I don't bother to correct her. There's no use. Telling her what happened with Chris will only cause another argument I'm not willing to have right now. So instead, I redirect the conversation back to her.

"Seriously though, what are you gonna do when all this shit runs out?" I pop my thumb towards the back of the truck, indicating her reason for our current dialogue.

"Then I'll make it. If I'm forced to live out this hell we call life, then I will do it fuzzy. I don't want to be reminded every day, how this all happened and who I lost during its demise." Her tone leaves no room for discussion or argument, like every time before, that I've brought up the topic of her drinking. And guilt shreds my insides as if I just swallowed a handful of razor blades.

Bea killed her brother, who also happened to be her best friend and neighbor, to save my life, and if she doesn't want to remember, I'll do whatever it takes to ensure that she doesn't. Who am I to judge her and how she chooses to live? I will do laps around this whole fucking city to get this woman a shot of vodka, if that's what she wants. Whatever it takes to erase the look of pain and sadness that lines her eyes when she glances at me.

I never understood how she had something that was more important than survival during the apocalypse, but now I see that it wasn't more important than survival, but this was the only way she is surviving.

"We have one more stop," Bea says cautiously as if I don't already realize this. I know we have one more stop, and I dread this stop the most.

The hospital.

We try to stop at a medical facility of some sort to get whatever we can on every run, but no matter how much I plan it out, we always end up running for our lives.

I've mapped out the floor plan of this hospital and memorized it, same as every other medical facility for miles. I managed to download the basic layout online. There are still some sources of internet and electricity that run throughout the city. Satellites weren't affected, only those who controlled them.

With no one to govern it, it's basically a never-ending supply if you can tap into it correctly. I've had some outside help with that, not that I would tell anyone, but now we have access to a lot of things still available on the internet that can help us create a new life. Blueprints and how to's have come in extremely handy since the outbreak.

Sobering my thoughts and remembering what I came in for, I make my way through a narrow corridor to the supply closet in the hospital to gather the items from the small wishlist Dr. Tanner sent. Thanks to Rowan's crew, I make it in with no issues and begin loading my bag with as much as I can carry, starting with the most important.

Dr. Tanner had asked for a few larger pieces but we don't have the room to spare on this haul. We needed more food and clothing than ever due to all the new members of the community and this winter has been extra harsh on everyone.

I have all I can take and make my way back down the narrow corridor to the parking lot where Bea is waiting for me. She's no slouch on our runs but these hospital trips are dangerous and sketchy in the best of times, and she isn't as fast as she used to be. We need to have one driver and the other one to go fetch. It's the only way we can guarantee one of us always makes it back with the haul.

It's eerie walking through deserted places like this when you know it used to be so loud and full of commotion, but the only thing that greets you is silence. Even the smallest of noises echo off the walls with nothing to absorb it, so when a large crash comes from behind you, there is no mistaking that you're no longer alone.

I freeze but only for a brief second before my fight or flight reflexes kick back in. I just need to make it out of the building and I'm free from there. I do not need to fight anything or anyone off right now when we are this close to going home. Coming face to face with a human is almost as bad as coming face to face with a zombie as of late.

I pick up my speed without making too much sound and keep my back to the wall as I make my way through as fast as humanly possible. My heart pounds through my chest as panic tries to set in, but I fight it off knowing I won't make it out alive if I lose focus.

I come around the corner almost crashing into a horde of z's that are circling something, but I don't stop to see if I caught their attention. I spin on my heel and take off in the other direction towards where I hope Bea is waiting and ready to take off.

Crashing through the side door, I dart in the direction of the truck I can see idling about 100 metres away, when out of nowhere a tank comes at me followed by a sprinter. I stumble slightly in shock at its immense size and try to determine my odds of survival right now.

I don't have to think long before a shot sounds off and hits the tank in the leg, dropping it to its knees, and upping my chance of survival. Marginally.

Tanks are practically invincible. It's skin nearly

impenetrable and gunshots usually don't kill it, so by shooting its legs, you at least give yourself a running chance.

Forgetting about its extended reach, it grabs my ankle, tripping me up and throwing me off balance knocking me to the winter landscape. I let go of the bag of supplies and crash unceremoniously to the hard snow and ice, cutting my hands and the side of my face in the process.

Fuck that hurts.

I don't have time to dwell on my road rash, -ice rash?- and lurch to my feet, but not quickly enough. The sprinter hits me like a linebacker and takes me back to the ground forcing the rest of the air from my lungs in a cloud of smoke. He lunges forward, jaws open and clamps down on my shoulder. Hard. The force of his bite makes me scream out, but he doesn't breach my leathers.

Not today, Satan.

I shove him off of me as hard as I can and Bea takes the kill shot, right between the eyes. I don't hesitate as I scramble to my feet and run towards the truck, stumbling through the heavy drifts, leaving all the medical supplies behind.

Fuck! All that for nothing.

After we drive for about fifteen minutes, and my heart comes back to a normal pace, I pull down the passenger side mirror and scan the damage on my face. Large jagged cuts pull from the side of my cheek and down my neck. Some start as high as my eyebrow and cut across my face, marring its once flawless appearance. My blond hair is matted to my skin and tinted red from the blood.

Bea clears her throat and I already know the question before she even asks it, but know it's necessary none-theless. "You bit girl?"

I chuckle, trying to lighten the mood. "No, I wasn't bit. Thank fu—" Her head snaps my way so I correct myself quickly before earning a cuff upside the head. "Thank-fully...I wear my leathers. Nothing pierces the skin through these and the cold weather only aids it." I smirk, feeling proud that I pulled off my cover-up.

"Mhmmm." Bea just shakes her head in disapproval. She knows what I was going to say, but out of respect, I try not to curse around her. Same as you wouldn't drop the F bomb in front of your grandmother.

"Here, wipe your face. You've got some pretty deep gashes." She says while handing me a lemon-scented wet wipe that's probably been in her purse since the 80s. No joke. Although granted, they have come in pretty damn handy on quite a few of our "shopping" trips.

"I hate to say it, but we may have to find another medical facility to get some of that stuff the doc asked for. And now to patch you up. Jesus girl, I can't take you anywhere." She finishes while shaking her head and mumbling. I thought I heard something about he's gonna kill me when he sees your face, but I really can't be sure.

CHAPTER 2

Lucie

W e make it back to the compound without any other instances, including our unscheduled extra medical stop. With my hands and face all bandaged I definitely look worse than I feel, but can't take the chance of infection nowadays. Due to my current state, I had to give driving privileges to Bea, which in turn took us an extra day to get home. Bea hates driving, especially in the winter, and now that we have to plow our way through the snow, she is even less fond of it.

With my hands like this, it will give me extra time to map and document everything that happened on this trip. This is the first time I've come in contact with a tank anywhere near the city like that. I'm gonna have to message Rowan immediately to extra take precautions in the city confines, and let him know I didn't get the supplies this time for his group. He doesn't have a huge community like we do, but he has a small group that has taken control of an apartment building on the outskirts of the city, with limited outside access.

If we're getting these breeds this close, it won't take

long before they're making their way north to our neck of the woods. I will also have to let Lochlan know what I encountered so he and the security team are prepared. Granted, we seem to have less z's in the winter, but the weather will be changing soon enough and that makes traveling easier. For both zombies and humans alike. And sometimes, one is no better than the other.

As we pull up to the gates of the compound, I can practically feel the tension looming over the area like a heavy fog. More men than normal are posted out front, and I've seen tire tracks for what looks to be a lot of vehicles coming and going. Recently. We've only been gone a few days, but something is different. I can feel it.

We nod to everyone as we drive through our makeshift town and head towards the warehouse drop off when we see Lochlan loading up an ATV with equipment.

"That can't be good if he's taking fencing material." Bea points out quietly, and I couldn't agree more. It either means we had a fence breach or he is having to cage something to keep from the rest of the population. Either way, he looks pissed to be doing whatever it is he is having to do and I make a mental note to steer clear of him for a while.

Lochlan is the head of our security here, and rightfully so. He's ex-military, strong, impenetrable and downright ruthless. He can make the call most others can't; the choice of life or death. People call him an asshole -and don't get me wrong, he is- but for the wrong reasons.

When the outbreak started, no one was safe out there, no matter who you were. No matter how much firepower you thought you had, there were always more infected. Their numbers supersede ours by hundreds of thousands, possibly millions, and it grows daily making humanity the minority. He is the one who approves all new community members and deems those worthy and removes those who are not. Just because you show up here looking for refuge, doesn't mean you'll get to stay.

He seems to have this ability to sense people's intentions and I've witnessed first hand how on point his intuition is. He has saved us all, countless times over by making those types of calls, so when Lochlan makes a call on behalf of our community's safety, I for one stand behind it faultlessly.

Watching the gates of the warehouse roll up, I can't help the small burst of butterflies that set flight in my stomach at the chance of seeing Chris. I know he was a dick to me before I left, but after what happened on our run, I could use a little of his tyrannical behaviour right now. I'm almost positive that makes me a masochist, but the desire to be near him is there nonetheless.

However, it's Dante that stands in the empty space smiling, and waving us through to offload instead. The truck barely has time to slow before he is ripping open my door to no doubt give me a bear hug and raz me for something. These boys are like the brothers I never had, and the ones I wished I could have been given. Instead, I was blessed with foster brothers who enjoyed a more *physical* approach to their torture. One that left emotional scars instead of visible evidence.

The door being pulled open rips me from my wayward

thoughts, revealing my current condition to Dante and he stops dead in his assault, freezing mid-air with a concerned and shocked expression.

Bea and I have been doing these runs for what seems like forever, and never have I returned in a condition quite this bad. Don't get me wrong, we've had runs-ins and injuries before, but none that have looked as bad as my current wounds.

My hands look like lobster claws wrapped in thick gauze with a matching headdress to stanch the bleeding until we could make it back. It didn't seem bad at the time, the cold weather slowing the bleeding, but after I warmed up a bit in the truck, the gash on my head and the multitude of cuts across my palms, wrists and face began to drip uncontrollably. Realistically, I could probably have used a few stitches, but I think the time frame for repair has lapsed.

"What the fuck happened?!" His shout echoed throughout the massive warehouse-like building, garnering everyone's attention within it. His hands come up to cradle my head and he begins to tilt it gently back and forth, surveying the damage and acting as though he's searching for the culprit in its confines.

"She's fine! Now somebody help my old ass out of this godforsaken truck! I've been stuck in it sober, for two days too many," Bea demands, thankfully not making a big deal out of my injuries and drawing more attention to herself than me. But Dante doesn't take the bait and levels me with a hard stare.

"It looks worse than it is. Honest," I say while holding

up the symbol for scout's honor. Or at least I think it is. Shit, I could be showing the international sign for the shocker for all I know, but he seems to accept it either way.

"Seriously Luce, what happened?" His true concern evident in his voice now as he watches me closely.

"Just a small run-in with a tank and a sprinter when we tried to get some of the hospital supplies. Which is also why we weren't able to get as much this time around." My voice sad at my own admission, because everyone counts on us to provide the things they need most and I failed.

It doesn't happen often, but it bothers me more than it should when it does. I've never had anyone rely or depend on me before coming here, and something inside me thrives off it. So when it does happen, I always make sure to get twice as much on the next run, but it doesn't lessen the guilt when someone suffers or goes without because I wasn't able to get it.

"I think you should go see Dr. Tanner right away, just to be safe. Lord knows we don't need your crazy ass running around all hopped up on the Z." He laughs at his own words, instantly lightening the dark territory our conversation was heading.

"I'm fine, honest—" But he holds his hand up to cut off any protest I might have about going to get checked out, and truth be told, he's right. I did a pretty decent cleanup job, but that doesn't mean I'm in the clear. So rather than argue a losing battle, I just nod in mock defeat.

"Fine! Can you at least back up and help me down so that I can go see Dr. T?"

Dante's big hands grab me under the arms and help lift me out of the truck and plants my feet on the concrete floor. He reaches up and grabs my backpack that I never go anywhere without and loops it over my shoulder.

"Hurry on over to the clinic Luce, you'll want to be seen sooner rather than later." He finishes with a small smile that seems just a little too cheery for telling me to go to the hospital, but I ignore it as he seems to have his attention pulled elsewhere.

I scan the warehouse one last time to see if I can see Chris, but I come up empty-handed, so I make my way to the clinic across the community square, furthest from the gates.

When I step inside, my senses are invaded by the pungent smell of cleaner and sickness. The need to gag is overwhelming and I have to breathe through my mouth a few times to choke it down. I hate hospitals and everything about them. I spent way too much time in them as a child, that the only thing stepping in here does is bring back terrifying memories that will take me weeks to rid myself of.

When Heidi sees me and my state of injury she jumps to her feet and comes rushing forward, her arms outstretched, but seems to realize her mistake and stops a few feet in front of me.

"Have you been bitten child?" she asks quietly as though it will be our little secret if I were.

"No, I'm not bitten, just stumbled while trying to get

away." I see her face pale at my words and that's the kiddy version of what happened. I could just imagine the hissy fit she would have if she heard the reality of the situation.

"It looks worse than it really is, I promise." I try to reassure her as much as possible but I can tell she ain't buying it. She's been working as a nurse since the seventies, I bet she's heard and seen more stories and lies than I could ever hope to dream up, so I don't even try.

"Well, come here and give us a hug, love. It's always nice to see you, even if it is under these circumstances. We don't get many people visiting when they aren't sick," she says it so solemnly, that I make a mental note to bring her some baked goods or something and visit her while I'm home. Just because.

After she's done showering me with affection, which I enjoy too much, she brings me back to an examination room, passing many empty ones along the way. However, there is one that isn't empty and the person occupying it is not someone I recognize.

As I get closer, I try to peek in but at the last second I catch a glimpse of Chris sitting next to her bed, laughing along with her.

Who is this woman and why is Chris with her? Why are they laughing?

I can feel my thoughts begin to spiral out of control and jealousy begin to take hold at the sight of Chris sitting with a strange woman. A woman I've never met. A woman he can't have known long. A woman that isn't me.

I know we aren't together and I don't have any claim

on him, but it doesn't lessen the pain at seeing how carefree he is with her. How he doesn't seem tense or irritated like he does around me. No, he seems to enjoy being in her presence, unlike any time we've spent together.

As though he sensed my scrutiny, his head turns and locks his eyes on mine, causing me to stumble ever so slightly.

"Oh no love, are you okay?" Heidi asks, concerned that my stumble has more to do with my state of health as opposed to my state of sanity. If only she knew how not ok I really am right now. Unable to answer her, I just nod and smile, urging her to continue to the room before I do something to embarrass myself in front of he who should not be named and his new *girlfriend*.

God, I know I sound childish, and I can see how ridiculous my thoughts are, but I don't care. There are very few things in this world that I cherish and even fewer people. And Chris is one of them. Ya, we fight like brother and sister, but it doesn't feel the same when we get along. We have this closeness that I've only ever felt with him and I refuse to give that up.

Thankfully I'm shut away in a private exam room while my head drags me through hell and back as I wait for the doctor to come and assess the damage.

I take the time to reflect on everything that's happened out there over the past couple of days and determine a way to inform everyone of what went down without causing a panic. Bea and I never tell anyone the full extent of our missions or what lengths we go to in order to procure and provide for this community. We dumb down our missions to everyone, well, everyone except Lochlan. He knows the truth of what we deal with and how dangerous it is.

Lochlan was the one to suggest we keep our rendezvous PG13 to the public, but not so much as to lead them into a false sense of security, and let them believe they are capable of doing what we do themselves. Chances are, anyone else would not have survived today and it was a close call as it was.

"Hey Lucie, I hear you had a little fall?" Dr. Tanner comes in looking down at my chart but smiles full watt when she glances up at me. No doubt because I was able to grab a few of her "must-have" items on the list, thanks to our extra stop, even though the equipment was a no go. I told her before we left I wasn't sure I would be able to get it this shipment, and that this was more of a trial run to see what our options were.

"Ya, just a little fall." I don't bother to stop the sarcasm that bleeds into the tone of my voice, because yet again, nobody needs to know the truth about how close it really was today.

Too close.

"Well, let's take a look and see what we can do to stitch you up and send you on your way. No bites right?" she asks as if I was hiding something while guiding my back down on the gurney. Jeez, do I look that bad that everyone keeps asking if I was bitten?

"No bites Doc. Just a few cuts and bruises, and making sure to follow protocol." I smile and close my eyes while she unravels my amateur patch job around my head and let her do her thing.

I don't bother to open them again until she taps my arm and says she's done. It was only 20 minutes but I somehow managed to fall asleep during that time. It's rare to get a moment of reprieve where you don't have to worry about being eaten or attacked in your sleep, from both humans and zombies alike. Apparently my body recognized the opportunity and took advantage of it.

Surveying my newly repaired wounds, I take notice of the stitches that now line the meaty part of my thumb, shocked at not realizing she was even doing it.

Jesus, was I drugged? How did I not feel that?

When I reach up, I feel matching stitches in my hairline just below my forehead and chuckle lightly, making a mental note so I don't rest my goggles there and tear em out when I pull them down.

I don't wait for Dr. T to say anything after I thank her, I just grab my stuff and make my way back the way I came in, hoping to catch a glance at Chris. I don't really want to talk to him at the moment, but I can admire from afar without having him open his mouth and ruin it.

Disappointment settles over me when I realize he isn't there anymore and I catch myself almost sulking at the fact I didn't get to see him.

Shit, I feel like one of those girly teenagers pining after her high school crush you see on an after school special. Ain't nobody got time for that. It's the fucking apocalypse and the last thing I need is to get my hopes up on a future that is technically non-existent at this point.

Something I've clearly built up in my head to mean more than it does.

Shaking off the desperate thoughts of Chris, I pull myself together and head out the front and go straight to the house I share with Bea. No doubt she's already half corked, so it gives me the time to document everything to send a message to Rowan before one of his group gets attacked by that tank. We didn't kill him, just immobilized him and he needs to be aware.

CHAPTER 3

CHRIS

Lucie is supposed to be back today, causing my body to thrum with anxious energy as the need to be near her courses through my veins. She's been gone almost four days, which is two days over their targeted time frame and three days too many if you ask me.

Lucie and Bea are our gatherers and have been doing these runs almost every week since they've been here, having to go further and further for supplies. Without them, we probably wouldn't have lasted this long. Sure we have supplies and have done well with growing and harvesting our own gardens and animals, but without them constantly running for medicine, household necessities and clothing, we would be in much worse shape at this point.

However, Lucie's role in my survival is vastly different than all the others. Since I was a child, I have suffered from anxiety and panic attacks. I had a service dog prior to the outbreak to help during the episodes, but unfortunately, he didn't survive the attacks. After that, I struggled more often than not, until the day I met Lucie.

Lucie has this extraordinary ability to surround me and settle my chaos without doing anything except existing. Lucie gets me at my worst and lowest times, baring the brunt end of my agitation. And as selfish as it is, I cling to that like a lifeline. Somehow, she makes me forget that we're surrounded by zombies, or that the entire world is falling to shit. She calms my anxiety like no medication ever could.

I need her.

Her quiet, her calm.

At this point, I'll take whatever she is willing to give me, and right now, I doubt that will be very much.

We didn't part on the best of terms when she left this time, my fault of course, but something about her makes me act impulsively, and never for the better. I always manage to come across as an asshole or an overbearing brother, no matter my intentions and it causes her to push away from me, causing my anxiety to spike until she can bring me back from my own edge of insanity.

So when my first glimpse of Lucie is her walking through the clinic, her head and both hands bandaged, blood seeping through the gauze, I lose my proverbial shit. I'm up and out of the exam room, leaving Adira stranded and confused at my outburst, but I don't give a rat's ass at this point. My mind a hurricane of concern and anger, spiraling out of control at seeing her hurt, even at the slightest cut or scrape, let alone a fucking head wound.

I feel my chest begin to tighten as the first signs of a panic attack begin to manifest. My breathing becomes laboured and my vision begins to swim slightly. I press my palm against the wall to help steady and ground myself as I attempt to pull myself together enough to get answers as to what happened to Lucie.

I know this makes me look weak, but no one understands. They don't realize what Lucie does for me, what she means to me. They all believe it's just a crush or an obsession to fuck her, but that couldn't be further from the truth. Lucie is, well… she's fucking Lucie! Lucie is my world. My end all, be all. I don't know, I can't explain it, and every time I try I get the same response, so I gave up trying and just keep that piece of her to myself.

"Someone else needs to get here, now, and take Adira back to her cell!" I shout over the radio system to the other security team members while fighting my own body for control of my breathing. And based on the stars slowly circling my head, I'm losing the battle.

"What's up, lover boy, gotta check on your injured girl?" I hear Dante spew in response with humor in his voice, sending a wave of nausea through me. He fucking knew this was gonna happen. Chances are, the fucker already saw her at the warehouse before she was forced to come to the clinic and he didn't say anything or give me a heads up to prepare myself.

"Fuck you, D!" I growl at him in irritation. They know what I'm like when it comes to Lucie, but he still taunts me anyway.

He doesn't say anything, but his cackle radiates through the radio like it's on surround sound, making me grind my teeth so hard, I'm pretty sure I heard one crack. He thinks this is funny, but it couldn't be further from it.

We can't take the chances we used to before the outbreak. One cut, one infection going untreated, is all it takes for a human to switch sides from the living to the undead, and I for one won't allow that to happen to Lucie.

Ever.

"Anyone know where the fuck Bea is?" But I don't wait for their response this time, as I storm through the clinic and outside heading towards her house. Anger must exude from me because every person I pass by keeps their eyes down and quickly moves from my path of destruction.

When I make it to their home, I don't bother to knock, I just bust in and see Bea sitting in a worn-out chair, with a glass of amber liquid in her hand. She doesn't flinch or even react at my disheveled appearance, just continues to swirl the glass's contents as though it has her hypnotized.

"Christopher, I see the assassins have failed again," she sneers, with a slight slur to her voice. I know they haven't been home long, so how is she this sloshed, this quick?

"What the actual FUCK, Bea? I just saw Lucie at the clinic, and she is all bandaged up with blood oozing from head wounds. What the fuck happened? Was she bit?" My words rush out in a string of questions, not giving her time to answer as my emotions get the best of me.

"I trusted you to keep her safe and you let this happen!" I pace back and forth in front of her chair, raking my fingers through my hair and tugging on the short strands I'm able to latch onto.

"Listen here, you little shit. I will protect that girl from anything bad, with everything I have. *Including* you. So don't come at me when you have no idea what happened or what went down out there." Her voice like gravel, her comment meant to strike a nerve, hits home and my stomach drops out.

"Then fucking tell me! Explain it!" I scream at her as my arms flail around at my uncontrolled temper.

"We had a deal, Bea."

When Bea realized I had genuine feelings for Lucie beyond what everyone speculated, she pulled me aside and told me something that turned my world upside down, more so than the apocalypse itself.

Turns out, Lucie is only sixteen. Well, seventeen, almost eighteen now, which Bea likes to hang over my head and remind me of every chance she gets. Bea also threatened me within an inch of my life that if I ever touched her in a way that isn't PG, she would cut my balls off and feed them to me. I know she's old and all, but shit, I think she meant it.

The moment I knew her age, everything I felt towards her was wrong, tainted almost, but I still wasn't willing to give it up. My frustration builds the longer I have to stay in check, keeping my hands to myself and not claim her as my own, living with me where I can keep her safe.

In any case, we agreed that until Lucie was legally *allowed* to be mine, she would protect her with everything she had until it was my turn to care for my girl. No harm would befall her while she was with either of us. Lucie came first.

No matter what.

This was the only way I would agree to let Lucie continue to do these runs with Bea on a regular basis. So seeing her return in less than perfect condition under Bea's care sent me over the edge.

Before I can say anything more, Bea is up and out of her chair so quick, I barely register her movements. She steps right in my face, her jaw ticking in agitation. I won't lie, I'm nervous as hell right now. I've heard stories of what Bea is capable of, and I don't want to be on the receiving end of her ire.

"Don't. Tell me what to do. Come at me like that again and you'll be eating through a straw for the rest of your numbered days. You hear me, boy? And if you want to know something, man up and go ask her yourself." She emphasizes each word with a stab of her bony finger into my chest.

"I tried that once. I asked her about the leathers, *like you said*, and she got pissed at me and kicked me out!"

"Ya, I'm gonna bet it's the delivery she got pissed about, not the question. She has a real low tolerance for assholes and their bullshit." She chuckles as she settles herself back into the recliner she once salvaged from her old home, basically dismissing me.

Fuck.

She's not wrong and all that does is piss me off more.

I'm not sure I can handle this. Her going out and continue doing these runs. I thought for sure it would get easier after a year, but the longer she's away from me, the worse it gets.

The worse *I* get.

And to be honest, I'm not sure how much more I can take.

"She'll be back soon if you want to stick around and try again, lover boy?" Bea chuckles a dark sound as she takes pleasure in my demise.

I turn on my heel and storm out the front door, making a beeline to my own place. I can't hit Bea, I know that, but fuck do I want to. I swear some days that old broad gets a kick out of everyone's misery. Shit, maybe it's just mine, but she thrives on it either way.

I storm into my own house, practically kicking the door off of its hinges and make my way upstairs to take a cold shower and cool off. I knew the possible consequences of these runs, but I never imagined it would ever actually happen. There have been some close calls here and there and a few scrapes and bruises, but nothing as bad as this.

Seething at the insufferable woman hell bent on making my life a living fucking nightmare, I just about rip my clothing to shreds trying to remove them in my haste to try and subdue the beast that's growing inside me.

I turn on the shower, not bothering to turn on the hot water tank and just let the freezing water run full tilt. Stepping under the spray I barely notice the frigid temperatures and try to focus on calming my nerves.

Inhale.

Exhale.

Inhale.

Exhale.

I do that a few more times until I feel like I have my

temper and mind calmed enough for me to focus my thoughts.

Seeing her like that really fucked me up and I can't seem to grasp any semblance of control. I wanted nothing more than to scoop her up, and bring her back here, strip her down and ensure she was safe and ok. To wrap my arms around her and inhale her sweet scent of lavender and innocence.

I groan as my cock begins to stir at the thought of stripping Lucie and her alluring scent. I reach down and squeeze it, trying hard to quell the hard-on that has decided to pop-up at the mere thought of Lucie. I know it's wrong and I shouldn't be thinking of her like this, but every time I get in here, it's a losing battle. I hate myself for it every time, but it doesn't stop it from happening. The more I realize how wrong it is to have these thoughts, the harder I seem to get.

Fuck it.

I reach down and stroke my shaft, giving it one long pump as I picture Lucie's perky tits as she sits atop me. I have to brace myself on the tile wall as the feeling of euphoria slams into me at the sight.

I close my eyes and allow myself to be swallowed by the fantasy of Lucie while I continue my self abuse. I know the regret and self loathing will come later when I realize what I've done but right now, I don't have the willpower to stop it.

The next morning starts out no better than how the day before ended, as the security team is called to the station for a meeting. Lochlan didn't say why, but my guess, it's in regards to the fence break and what Adira informed us of and what our next move will be.

Making my way into the station, my thoughts are on what I can do to keep Lucie safe, and if I can talk her out of doing any more runs, when I come to a screeching halt. There standing in the entranceway talking to Tripp, is my kryptonite wrapped in leather. I wasn't prepared to see her this morning, and I'm thrown off-kilter at the sight of her.

Lucie is every guy's wet dream. A blonde *Lara Croft*, cocooned in leather. Thick pieces strategically placed, enhancing her thin waist and thick thighs, goggles framing her porcelain face like a steampunk goddess. Her long winter coat hangs open, drawing attention to her pert tits that are currently encased in a bodice that is very form-fitted.

Just looking at her caused my dick to jerk towards her in my jeans, as the memories of my activities from last night bombard me. I try to adjust myself discreetly at the building pressure behind my zipper, but it's becoming harder to hide by the second. Pun intended.

Baseball. Cold showers. My grandma. Baseball. Bea.

I'm bumped from behind, my thoughts effectively halted at the interruption and I swing around ready to tell whoever they are to fuck off. When I realize it's Bea, the words die on my lips at her appearance. She looks just as bad as I feel, and I know she didn't sleep last night either. Probably replaying whatever scenario caused Lucie's injuries, and I'm betting her self loathing is doing a better job than any guilt trip I could throw at her right now, so I let it go.

And then she opens her mouth.

"Christopher, still alive I see." Bea sighs in disappointment as she sidles up to stand next to me observing the same person who has captured my attention.

Taking back all my previous thoughts, I'm just about to tell Bea where to go, when Lochlan's booming voice shakes the building in annoyance and saves me from pissing more people off as he bellows from the conference room door.

"Let's go, ladies!" he says while holding my stare.

Prick.

"Hey Lochlan, why do I gotta be here?" Lucie asks with teenage attitude laced in her tone as she hangs up her coat and makes her way over to stand next to us. She doesn't look at me, nor does she say anything and I watch as Bea takes in our encounter -or lack thereof- with a suspicious eye.

Lochlan turns back around, stomping toward us with a menacing look on his face ready to snap, and automatically I take a protective step in front of Lucie, casually blocking her from his direct line of sight, and placing myself between them. If I didn't know better, I would say a look of respect crossed his face at my action, but it was so fast, it could have just been wishful thinking on my behalf.

I know Adira has got him riled up more than I have ever seen him before, and no one seems to know why, but

I won't let him or anyone else for that matter, talk to Lucie like that.

"Because, *Adira* is supposed to give us some intel about zombie breeds and what to expect, and since you and Bea have the most experience dealing with them on a regular basis, I would like you there, to correct any *incorrect* facts and offer any of your own." He softens his voice ever so slightly towards Lucie, catching my eye as if to say, *better?* and turns and heads towards the conference room with Bea now in tow.

"Who the hell is Adira?" Lucie questions innocently, not really directed at anyone, having no clue as to what's been going on since she left.

"Adira showed up not that long after you left. She says she's here to warn us that people are coming to take our supplies and whatever else. Our fences were cut the other day as well, so I think Lochlan is starting to take her seriously. He has a real hate on for her for some reason, and doesn't trust a word she says," I tell her, trying to fill in the missing pieces she is unaware of.

"You think she's telling the truth?" Lucie snides. I fight my smile at the jealousy that rolls off of her tongue as her face flushes in anger. I love watching the colour rise from Lucie's cheeks, and down her neck. I wonder if it goes all the way down when she flushes from arousal?

A clearing throat snaps me from my fantasy as I'm brought back to the current conversation, having to adjust myself again at the direction my thoughts were taking me.

"Ya, I do. I mean, she seems pretty honest and

sincere," I say with a shrug. Which, according to her reaction was apparently the wrong answer.

"Are you guys best friends now?" Her words are harsh and angry but a hint of vulnerability laces them. I can't help but shake my head at her ridiculous behaviour, but enjoy her reaction all the same. As much as her covetous attitude isn't warranted in the slightest, inwardly I thrive off the feeling knowing she feels this way because of me. She is jealous of someone else, over me.

Don't get me wrong, never would I hurt her in any way or cause her to doubt for a second I wouldn't be everything she ever needed of me, but it's reassuring that maybe my feelings aren't one-sided.

But I don't get the chance to say any of that before Lucie storms off towards the conference room and stops to speak with Bea and Lochlan in the doorway. I walk past all of them and make my way inside, my mood plummeting further as I continue to dig my own grave with Lucie.

I don't know how the fuck we got here. I feel like ever since that day Bea told me to talk to Lucie myself and to stop coming to her for everything, nothing has been the same. I get why she told me to go right to the source, but I feel like since then, there's this enormous strain on our once amicable relationship.

I asked Bea to talk to Lucie about her using a gun instead of that bat so she wouldn't have to get as close to make the kill. Bea's response,

"She had that thing, long before the apocalypse boy. Ya, let that sink in a little. You poke fun and laugh at her

clothes and weapon of choice, well maybe next time ask her why she chose that bat? Why she dresses the way she does? You give her shit, yet you can't seem to stay away from her and then make her *feel bad about it. You punish her whenever* you *get too close and things go too far and then pull away, leaving her reeling and me to pick up the pieces."*

"You toy with that girl's feelings to get what you claim you need from her, but at what cost? She is more fragile than you could ever know or imagine. Not that she would ever tell you that. Tell me, Christopher, what kind of relationship could you possibly have with that girl if you can't even talk to her and ask questions about her and her life? You don't even know that girl."

Our last encounter plays over and again in my head, drowning out the conversations currently taking place around me, plaguing me with horrible thoughts and scenarios. But the sound of Lucie's laughter pulls me out of my affliction and my gaze instantly finds her and the source that was able to elicit the sound only meant for my ears.

Lochlan.

Why the fuck is she laughing at Lochlan? He isn't funny. I cross my arms over my chest and glare towards the hulking man as he takes his seat at the head of the table, opposite Adira, oblivious to my scowl.

I block out the noise around me and focus solely on Lucie. I don't like fighting with her, and I don't like that she won't look at me. It's taking every ounce of strength in my body not to go over there and make her look at me.

Make her ease the ache that's forming in my chest at the wall she's put up between us and ease whatever is causing her worry. Lucie has never shut me down like this before and I hate it. I hate that she is ignoring me and paying attention to everyone else.

Completely wrapped up in my own thoughts, I hadn't even realized the meeting started and Adira's already halfway through the different breeds of zombies before my mind clears enough to hear what's being said around me. Adira begins speaking about "tanks" and I watch as Lucie's face pales instantly and bile rises in my throat.

I'm almost positive she's encountered one of these before, based on the fear plainly displayed on her delicate features, pushing my anxiety to a near breaking point. It's always bothered me that Lucie goes out on these runs, and I can't settle until I know she's back and still human, but knowing that she's already privy to *this* knowledge, first hand, in order to provide for everyone, makes me feel sick.

"What about Demon Z's?" Lucie's singsong voice cuts through my nausea. Her nonchalant tone at something so volatile sounding is what sends me over the deep end, causing what little I had left of my self-control to snap. No longer do I possess the ability to hold back, as my body begins to shake with possessive energy.

"I'm sorry, what did you just say?!" My statement comes out harsher than I intended, making me sound annoyed and disbelieving, but I'm struggling to keep myself in check and not lash out at the fact she knows ANY of this shit.

Everyone's head snaps in my direction surprised at the tone I used towards Lucie. Myself included. Most, if not all of them know how I feel towards Lucie and what I can be like around her or what I am like when it comes to her safety. And if they don't know, they suspect.

Suddenly, every selfish favour I've asked of Lucie flashes in my mind. All those times she shrugged it off while Bea gave me the death stare when I asked for a particular item. I put her in situations where she may have to face some of these monsters.

I did it.

I should be mad at myself, but right now, I'm more furious with Lucie that she ever agreed to do it in the first place. And how many others does she do these favours for? How often is her life in danger because of this? I glance around the table at everyone in loathing, their clothing that she sacrificed her safety to obtain for them. I'm furious with Grey for his extra trip to his old home for family photos, and at Lochlan's extra trip for something from his home, and I'm angry at the entire community for demanding this of her.

Each time she leaves the compound I risk losing her, I know this, but hearing these things, and her corroborating stories is breaking me apart from the inside out. But it's Bea's graphic detail about what a demon z is that causes my whole body to react violently. My arms and legs shake with restrained fury, my fingers ache in protest while white-knuckling the arms of my chair, but no one seems to notice my internal breakdown. No one except Lucie.

She stares right at me as my mood becomes toxic, my

emotions running wild and uninhibited. I'm about to demand she never go on a run again, that she never, ever leave my side and effectively ruining any relationship I could ever hope to possibly have with her. But before I have the chance to single-handedly destroy my own future, the alarm indicating approaching danger blares through the station and everyone scatters like roaches, grabbing weapons and ammunition. I hear Adira beg Lochlan for a weapon but he refuses and makes his way to the back where we keep back up ammo.

Fucking idiot.

The mirrored expression clearly written across Grey's face shows that I'm not the only one thinking this, and I'm almost positive Lochlan is too, but his emotions are getting in his way and starting to cloud his judgement.

Like I'm one to fucking talk.

We need all the help we can get right now, and his stubbornness might actually get someone killed. Or worse.

CHAPTER 4

Lucie

T he whole station moves in a well-choreographed
dance as they prepare for battle. Some grabbing
guns, others ammo while the rest suit themselves up to
cover as much skin as possible. From what it sounds like,
this is no small group of z's coming in and they need to be
prepared for the worst, while I'm forced to sit back and
watch them go to war, so to speak.

I hate being left behind when I could help, but I know
why I am not allowed to help during these situations and I
can't fault their argument. They can't afford to *not* have
me around. That's not to sound cocky, but a proven fact.

Each of us in the community has a roll, and mine is to
provide for the others and ensure our survival. Sure, Bea
can do runs without me, hell anyone here can, but no one
has the knowledge of the cities like I do. No one can navigate the streets and buildings as I can. NO ONE can get
into medical facilities and make it out unscathed like I
can. And for that reason alone, I'm required to stay behind
when shit hits the fan.

But it doesn't make it easier to watch as Chris is

rushed out the door, strapped head to toe in tactical gear to meet our threat head on. Thankfully, this is not an everyday occurrence and less so in the winter, but it doesn't lessen the anxiety that builds inside me at the thought he might not return alive. Or that he returns *undead*.

I stand in the doorway watching as everyone that is stationed to do so, makes their way towards whatever danger is presenting itself. I can't see what's happening from here, but the sounds of shouting and random gunshots bounce off the buildings in the dense winter snow, amplifying the sounds of horror.

As I stand helpless waiting for everyone to return safely, a flurry of movement catches the corner of my eye, setting me on high alert. Not having time to warn anyone else, I grab my chain wrapped bat and dart after whatever it was that took off this way. If it's a sprinter and manages to get in behind the group currently fighting, they won't stand a chance of fighting against both fronts.

The wind whirls in anger as the temperature continues to drop, making my whole body shudder. I didn't have time to grab my coat before taking off after whatever was lurking around and I know I'm gonna regret it afterwards. The snow picks up speed and increases in size, reducing my visibility significantly. Ensuring I don't catch my stitches, I lift and drop my goggles to keep my vision clear of the ever falling flakes and lift my bandana to keep my face and lungs from freezing.

Canadian winters are no joke, and without proper protection from the elements, you will not survive. Simple as that. Frostbite, hypothermia, any of those are deadly when untreated and nowadays, those who die, tend not to stay that way. We can't afford any more undead wandering around. We're already outnumbered and that percentage increases daily.

When I make it around the corner, I come to a screeching halt as I take in the scene around me. Blood has coated the snow like a crimson blanket of both red and black. Gunshots are fired with insane accuracy, leveling the undead on the opposite side of the fence where the rest are trying to file through.

That's when I see Adira. With a sword in hand, she stands posted at the fence slicing through the undead army like warm butter. Those gathered, see the same thing I do and stare in amazement as Adira single-handedly eradicates ninety percent of the z's. She wields the sword like it was made for her, like another extension of her being. And for all I know, it was.

Wait—is that Chris's sword? Why is she using Chris's sword? I got him that sword! I risked my ass to get him that sword and he just hands it off to her as though it means nothing to him.

I know now is not the time to be self-conscious or worry about something so menial, and I shouldn't be upset. I *should* be happy that she's saving a lot of lives right now, including my own, but I can't get past the fact she is in possession of something that almost cost me my life to acquire for *him*.

Annoyance flares in me at both myself and Chris, as I fall back into the darkness created by another's shadow. I hate that he holds this power over me and my emotions. Hate that he still treats me like a younger sibling no matter what I do, still pushing me away every time it feels like we get close, but mostly I hate that I really don't hate it at all.

I like the feelings that he evokes within me, or what he elicits when he gets near me. I like the rush I get when I know I'm going to see him, and the butterflies I'm forced to fight off every time we end up somewhere alone.

With my focus solely on Chris and what he does to my head, I don't seem to register the sheer violence that is caused by Adira, but the moment she stumbles and the horde of undead leap forward at her disadvantage, I snap to reality and ready myself to join the mass of thrashing bodies to defend everything we've worked so hard for.

The rest of our army showers the group of infected with bullets, all hitting their marks with precision. Adira kips to her feet and doesn't hesitate a moment before hacking back into the fray of flesh as the infected still swarm her.

Out of nowhere, that same blur of movement from earlier captures my attention, and dread sets in the moment I realize the trajectory.

"ADIRA! BEHIND YOU!" I scream as loud as I can, cupping my mouth to project my voice as much as possible over the sounds of battle. In that same moment, I hear the echo of someone else shouting at the same time, partially drowning out my own warning, but it's too late.

The sprinter leaps on Adira and bites her shoulder,

causing me to gag at the sight of her flesh and whatever else, being torn away from her body.

Fear propels me forward, ready to aid in the fight and give Adira a chance to recover and fight back, but the damage is done. I've seen it all before. She doesn't have long now.

From out of nowhere, a bullet goes through the zombie's head that has bitten Adira and brain matter leaks from its fresh wound. I look at Lochlan, wondering why he shot the zombie and not Adira, but he seems just as shocked and confused as I am.

I don't have time to dwell on it, because a Z comes up behind me and tackles me before I get the chance to defend myself. I bring my bat between us trying desperately to keep it from biting me, as drool, blood and whatever else drips from its mouth onto my face and I have to fight bile that's rising in the back of my throat. It leans over me, lunging forward desperate to make purchase, when flashes of Joe take its place. The snapping jaws, the look in Bea's eyes, all of it comes flooding back and I freeze up, giving it the opportunity it was looking for.

Pain rips me from my memories as my worst nightmare just became my reality. Again.

Shit! The fucker bit me.

A scream rips from my throat as fire sears my veins instantly and the poison pumps through my body faster with each rush of adrenaline. I shake uncontrollably, but I'm not sure if it's from the pain or the cold. My vision wavers in and out of focus, making my stomach roil. I feel someone come up beside me but I can't make out who it is. My lip trembles as I beseech death, praying to end it quickly because I can't take the fire that's raging inside me.

I brace myself for the final blow. The one that kills me and prevents me from becoming one of the undead, but it never comes.

Instead, I'm scooped up and braced against a soft chest as pain floods my system and begins to take its toll on my body. Attempting to control my now irregular heartbeat, I try to slow and match mine to theirs. I do the same with my breathing, hoping to stall the turning process and maybe give them time to stop the spread of the virus. But even as I think the words, I already know it's no use by the obvious signs showcasing that my entire being has been compromised. I can barely breathe as it is, my chest constricting in pain as my body attempts to fight off the toxins invading my system at a breakneck rate.

Whispers of encouragement break through my mental fog and I realize it's Adira who's holding me, protecting me. She barges through the hospital doors as another rush of pain shoots through me and I'm laid out on something flat and somewhat soft.

Wave after wave of heat engulfs every limb, making my back bow off the surface and agony like no other consumes me, causing my stomach to contract and folding me in half. Hunger pains force an unnatural growl from within me and I snap my eyes open in fear. They immediately land on a soft arm facing me, and I watch as the promise of life pumps furiously beneath the pale surface.

The need to taste it, taste her, overwhelms me,

prompting my senses to act on their own accord, and before I realize what I'm doing, I've leaned forward, taking her wrist in my grasp and inhaling her essence.

A shiver works its way up my spine at the delectable scent, but I don't stop there. I couldn't even if I wanted to. I use my tongue to trace a line from the top of her hand to the inside of her wrist, welcoming the taste she leaves behind.

Without warning or a conscious decision, I strike, sinking my teeth into Adira's wrist and breaking through her pliable flesh. A flavour so rich, so heady, invades my mouth and a sudden calm blankets me as a soothing coolness begins ebbing the inferno within.

Like an addict, I instantly crave it like nothing else I've ever wanted before. Energy skates along the surface of my skin, like a thousand live wires firing off at random. Zaps of electricity spark at the sensation of power being provided by the coppery substance as each swallow satisfies a deep hunger.

Gasps of horror and shock permeate the air around us as others file in and witness the feral side begin to take over. But all I can manage to do is stare at Adira in awe as I continue to consume her life source. She doesn't pull her arm away or balk at my actions but instead cups the back of my head as if to encourage me to continue.

Tears form in my eyes because I can feel her pain, her fear and her desire. I can see her light and the darkness that seeps into her soul. But I can also feel power. A strength like no other that resides inside her and I can feel it as I gulp down more of her.

She turns from me and shouts at someone in the room, but I can't hear a word. Fatigue is quick to settle in and my body is weakening and shutting down. Darkness calls to me, promising a reprieve from the agony and I go willingly as I'm pulled under its spell.

CHAPTER 5

CHRIS

I'm not exactly sure who helped me out of the snow, or who hauled my ass to the clinic and deposited me in a chair next to Lucie's bed, but I'm grateful they did.

I don't remember much after the alarm sounded, but one thing I won't forget is the sound of Lucie's ear-piercing scream echoing around me. The horror it contained as her voice ratcheted up in pain, brought me to my knees as fear immobilized me.

Lucie was bit.

Lucie was *fucking* bit, and I wasn't there to save her.

To protect her.

Emptiness consumed me and I stopped fighting. Dropping down into the snow and watching as my reason to fight was taken from me, left a void so large it swallowed me whole.

Adira, however, refused to give up Lucie's body when she was bitten, running back to the clinic and growled fiercely at anyone who came near her without intentions to help. Going against every protocol we have in place, Adira demanded that Dr. Tanner inject Lucie with her blood, claiming she contains some form of antidote. Silence descended upon the room at her declaration as this new revelation sank in, giving a sliver of hope no one dared to question.

Not even Lochlan.

And now, we all sit here in silence waiting on the outcome of a long shot, praying for miracles while Adira and Lucie lie unconscious, fighting to return to us.

If this works, Adira will have saved Lucie's life and become a living cure.

CHAPTER 6

Lucie

I'm alive.

At least I think I am. I can hear voices but can't make out a sound. Their words not clear enough to understand in my hazy mind, but I cling to them anyway.

I feel a squeeze on my hand and I try to squeeze back to assure whoever it is that I can feel them too, but nothing happens, nothing will cooperate. I can't open my eyes or make my body function at my command and fear begins to settle in.

I begin to silently panic at my paralyzed state and the room takes notice as the sound of the incessant beeping on the machine brings attention to my rapidly spiking heart rate. I hear a shuffle beside me and want to scream for help, but nothing fucking happens.

The beeping continues to speed up as I proceed to freak the fuck out, trapped in my unmoving body. When suddenly a cold sensation crawls up my arm and within seconds my anxiety recedes and a soothing blackness takes its place. I welcome the darkness and its comfort and embrace it like a mother's love as it whisks me into slumber.

CHAPTER 7

CHRIS

It's been three days since Lucie was bit, and three days I've lived in this darkness. My own personal hell surrounding me as she lies motionless. The longer we sit here, the more hope drains from my body and doubt settles in, weaving its mental torture through my exhausted brain.

I hold her hand and tell her things I've never said to her, things that I should have said long before this moment existed. I don't care how old she is, or who hears it, or what they think of it or us, because she needs to know what she's fighting for.

I know she can hear me, I can feel it. I just need her back. I need her to tell me she's alright so that I can be alright.

"How's she doing?" Bea's voice startles me from the door. She refuses to come inside the room, saying it will only make things more real.

Me? I haven't left her side once, only to use the washroom and only because it's attached to her room. Any further away and they would have to bring me a commode or hook up a catheter, because there is no chance in fucking hell that I am leaving her side.

"Honestly? I don't know. I thought for sure she would be awake by now. Adira has already woken up and is out and about helping fortify fences and fighting off attacks. Lucie hasn't even opened her fucking eyes yet." I lean forward on my elbows and pull the strands of my hair, positive I must be almost bald at this point, for how much I've been doing it lately.

"She'll wake up."

Her words sounded so convincing, so sure, but I couldn't latch onto the hope they were intended to instill as despair descends upon me in her ever-growing absence.

She's my light, my sunshine, my horizon in the darkness that is now our miserable existence and I'm not sure I can survive without her.

CHAPTER 8

Lucie

Silence greets me as the fog begins to lift. I'm not sure how long I've been out, but when I can finally open my eyes, I only want to close them again. The bright overhead lights make me hiss in pain as they cause my head to pound immediately. I lift my hands to cradle it and block out the offending glow, but when I do, I'm forced to knock another hand loose.

Looking down, I'm met with the most beautiful set of eyes I have ever seen and I take in my fill for what seems like the first time. Ocean blue, with flecks of gold and a green ring around the pupil, stare back at me in hope. Dark circles sit under their rich colours making his exhaustion more prominent.

Chris.

"Hey." His voice sounding like gravel. He tries to clear his throat but it still sounds the same, as though he hasn't used it in weeks. He sits up suddenly and flits about, trying to busy his hands. "How are you feeling?"

"I—" I try to speak, but nothing comes out, my mouth dry from the days of lack of use. Chris is out of his chair and in the hallway, shouting, "She's awake!" and "I need water stat!" before I have the chance to try again. I almost chuckle at his absurdity, but can't muster the energy.

Left alone as Chris tracks down some water, my eyes scan the room, unable to focus on one thing. Everything looks so different, yet the same. The colours are brighter, the fabric softer. I can't tell if it's because I've been absent from this stuff and it's like seeing it for the first time or because of the effects of the zombie bite.

A tear slips free at that thought, remembering what happened and my emotions begin to overwhelm me in an instant. Fear, anger, relief and about a thousand others clash, each fighting for sovereignty.

I reach up to touch the place where I was bitten, still tender, I grasp my arm and hiss as the pain amplifies at my touch. The traitorous machine beside me kicks into high gear, as my heart tries to escape the confines of my chest, thundering loudly against my ribs. I clutch my throat as my breathing begins to wheeze and my airway constricts, as I begin to panic.

I reach for the blanket and toss it off me, too hot and tempered to be confined, but as soon as I swing my legs over the side of the bed, a soft hand lands on my arm to stop me. I release a silent scream in response, my mouth still resembling a desert as I try to scramble away.

"Hey, hey, hey. It's okay. I'm not going to hurt you, I promise," Adira coos from beside me. I have no idea where the fuck she just came from or how I never noticed her before, but her words cause me to still for a moment allowing me to gather my bearings.

"There you go. Deep breaths. Just like that." She continues her siren song as I slowly match my breathing to hers.

"What happened? Did I die? Am I one of them?" I whisper as another tear escapes down my cheek. I know I can't be one of them as I can still form coherent words and thoughts, but that doesn't mean I am human either.

"No Lucie, you're not one of them. You're something different. Something stronger. Something powerful. And something everyone *and* no one wants." Her face shows relief but fear and guilt ride shotgun along with it. I'm confused by her contradictory statement, but before I have the chance to ask, Dr. Tanner walks in and effectively halts the conversation.

"Welcome back to the land of the living, Lucie," Dr. Tanner jokes, though no one seems to laugh but her. She at least has the decency to blush and feel embarrassed at her lame attempt for humour. I, for one, don't find anything remotely funny about my current situation. I have no idea what condition I fall under or what to expect now.

All I know is, what happened is not right or normal and I know that this is just the beginning.

CHAPTER 9

CHRIS

3 months later…

"We need to do more medical runs," I address the group, as this is my number one concern, just like every other meeting in the last 3 months.

Since Lucie was bit and Adira gave her her blood, stopping the transition process and making her into the same type of hybrid as Adira, Dr. Tanner has been running test after test on both of them, hoping to come up with some form of cure. And because of that, we are going through medical supplies faster than usual. Not to mention whatever the fuck is going on with Lucie and her new quirk.

"We've tried! No one can get close enough to get the supplies needed. I don't know how Lucie fucking did it man. You have to be a god damned ninja," Dante says, looking at Lochlan with a strange look on his face. Dante has been going on runs with Bea and some of the others as a stand in for Lucie, but it takes two crews to do the same job her and Bea did, and still we don't have enough.

This winter has been bad, taking its toll on everyone and causing us to go through more supplies than we originally anticipated. Not to mention, we've taken in more people since then, and had to ensure everyone was set up to survive.

"How is it that a seventy something alcoholic woman and a fucking teenage girl can feed, clothe and provide for an entire community, including medical supplies *and* equipment, but two grown men can't manage to get so much as a fucking bandaid?" I growl in frustration. I know it's difficult and I get what they do isn't easy, but come on, how bad could it possibly be?

"Fuck you, you little punk!" Bea spits at me as she flies from her chair, ready to lunge at me while Tripp and Grey hold her back.

"Do you have any idea how dangerous hospitals are? Or hell, even clinics these days?" Dante tosses in my direction, clearly privy to information that I seem to be in the dark about in this situation.

"You think you can do better? Come with me pretty boy, I'll show you what my girl does that no one else can," Bea throws out in her usual unenthusiastic tone towards me and I just shake my head at her nonsense.

"Come on, Christopher. Pfft, I bet you don't make it 24 hours." She taunts me further, trying to get a rise out of me, and shit if it ain't working.

"No skin off my back," she finishes with a shrug, as if the thought of me dying is no big deal. God, this fucking woman irritates the shit out of me and she knows damn well that if it wasn't for Lucie, I would have put her in her place months ago.

"I can't do it without her and you know it. The whole community has been suffering since you've decided to pull her away from collecting. This community relies on her and these runs. Even you," she directs at me while extracting herself from the meeting, but her statement was more geared towards Lochlan and his decision.

You see, after Lucie was bit, Lochlan pulled her from doing runs until we could be sure she was well enough to do them and to guarantee there were no damaging or lasting side effects. Adira assured everyone that Lucie is and would be fine, and swore up and down that it was all normal, but after three months, even she doesn't seem as convinced anymore.

There are a few major differences that everyone is aware of, between Adira and Lucie's transitions, and when we realized we weren't dealing with the exact same thing, we had to reevaluate the situation.

Adira didn't have that lengthy unconscious period like Lucie did, which Dr. Tanner has chalked up to the amount of morphine she was subjected to during her transition. But Lucie was out for almost a week and she didn't seem to bounce back as quickly either, according to Adira.

Adira also doesn't seem to weaken like Lucie does after a certain period of time or after expelling energy. In fact, Lucie seems weak more often than not, where as Adira is the opposite. I'm not even sure anyone has noticed it at this point, as everyone clings to the hope of what this could mean for the future, but I noticed it. I notice *everything* when it comes to Lucie.

Every time Lucie weakens, it seems to be at an almost dangerous level and we have to give her a blood transfusion to restore her energy. Whereas Adira only seems to weaken after being bitten.

I've started to wonder if Lucie is beginning to crave the transfusions or the blood itself, as though she's trying to sate a different kind of hunger. The timeframe between her transfusions is growing less and less. And Lucie is always at her strongest after a transfusion. I'm starting to believe that she is needing the blood in order to survive, unlike Adira.

No one else seems to realize this possibly monumental and life altering fact, and I don't plan to alert them of it yet. At least not until I can be sure.

When Lucie turned, she fed from Adira directly, before anyone was able to inject her with Adira's blood and antibodies, and maybe that has something to do with it? I mean, I'm totally reaching here with this idea, but can you blame me? At this point, anything could be possible. For fuck's sake, there are zombies running around.

Fucking zombies!

No one has tested this theory, yet as no one actually realizes what is happening to the full extent at this point. With everything that has been happening here lately, the fact she is alive is in the plus books, no one seems to really care beyond that.

But how would I even go about testing this theory? Shit, I don't even know if I have a theory, because I feel like I'm starting to go insane just thinking about this, but at this point, I'll try anything to help Lucie. Except, I have no idea where to even begin. It's not like she's a damn vampire and I could entice her with my blood or some shit.

Or can I?

CHAPTER 10

Lucie

Stepping out into the crisp night air I take a deep breath and inhale the calm created by the darkness. The daylight is not my friend these days, not that I can't go out in it, it's just too overwhelming, so when Chris suggested a late dinner, I was beyond grateful. Since my shift, my senses have been heightened, sunlight, loud noises and even people can create sensory overload, causing me to pretty much hole up indoors as much as possible. Not to mention, no one seems to want to be around me.

Well, no one but Chris.

Everyone has been nice and supportive since the incident, don't get me wrong, but that is about the extent of it. People fear the unknown, especially since the outbreak and I am no exception. The fact that no one knows why I weaken, or why I have sensitivities makes me "unpredictable, different, and unique" are the terms most often used, and people don't like different. Sure Dr. Tanner is nice, but to her, I'm more or less a science experiment until she can figure out why I'm weakening and how Adira's blood can help others.

But Chris is different. He doesn't shy from being in my presence like the others do. In fact, since I shifted, he is around me a lot more. Not that we never hung around before, but it was always in a mutual setting with other people, unlike tonight. This is the first time Chris has ever invited me over to his place and the first time we will be spending any definitive time alone together. To say I'm nervous is a severe understatement.

Butterflies take flight in my stomach at the reminder and it takes me a moment to reign in my emotions. The last thing we need tonight is for my system to crash and have to go see Dr. Tanner for another treatment. I just had one the other day and we are beginning to run danger-ously low on our blood supply, among other things.

Which is another reason he asked me over tonight. He said he has some questions about locations and supplies that might help the next crew to go out. Multiple teams have tried, but all seem to come up short of what Bea and I were capable of not long ago. I've helped as much as possible from the sidelines in anyway I possibly can, but it's not enough. They haven't been able to keep up with the demand since they benched me and now the commu-nity is beginning to suffer slowly. Our catalogue of supplies is dwindling down rapidly and no there is one to replenish it like before.

Last week, Lochlan was forced to turn away a few humans we found not far from the gates, due to lack of provisions, but if we don't do something soon, our own survival rate is going to diminish significantly.

I'm hoping this dinner tonight is the leaders coming to their senses and are letting me go back out again. But I definitely won't get my hopes up. It sounds more like a recon conversation more than anything.

I knock on his door and wait. I fidget while trying to chase the last bit of nerves and butterflies before I manage to make a fool of myself.

"Hey!" Chris says enthusiastically as he swings open the door, wearing a pair of grey track pants and tight white t-shirt that leaves nothing to the imagination. Ripples of muscle prominent through the fabric and making my inner sex kitten purr. I may not have a lot of sexual experience, but I don't need to when I have a great imagination.

I step inside and am immediately assaulted by the overwhelming scent of spices, musk and... Is that blood? Not the scent I'm accustomed to when it comes to Chris. Nor is it the smell of delicious food like I was expecting. The scent so powerful, invades my nostrils and I have to breathe through my mouth in order to tolerate it.

"You okay little one?" he asks, while I try to keep my shit together, concern evident on his face and laced in his voice. I hate the nickname he's assigned me, but I can't focus on that as I need to answer him before he gets suspicious of my reaction.

"Ya, I'm fine. Just a little tired," I say cautiously, gifting him a small smile and trying to casually shrug off his concern. I don't think he buys it, though he doesn't say so out loud. Instead, he just nods and holds his hand towards the living room.

"Make yourself comfortable. I'm just finishing up and we will be eating in a few minutes," he says backing away towards the kitchen I assume, as a weird tone takes over his voice. I probably wouldn't have normally noticed this, but like I said before, my senses are attuned to even the smallest of changes.

I can hear when he makes it back to the kitchen and starts mumbling to himself, but I can't quite make out the words as things are shuffled around and banged together. When his sudden shout of pain reaches my ears a moment after that, I don't hesitate taking off in the direction of the hall I saw Chris disappear down.

When my feet breach the threshold of the kitchen, I stop dead in my tracks, gripping the door frame to brace myself. Chris is on the other side of the counter, cradling his hand in what was once a white cloth, now stained red. My body reacts immediately and I stumble forward at the sight of Chris's blood.

I've never told anyone how affected I was from the zombie bite or Adira's blood and the process after. Everyone got the version I wanted them to have, but nobody knows the truth. The haunting reality of what I truly go through on a regular basis. The sensitivity to normal everyday things, cravings for things I shouldn't want, the hunger pains from my body not getting what it needs. And right now, is no exception.

I can smell the fresh blood from where I stand, feet firmly planted as far from Chris as possible. Frozen in fear at the thought that I may not be able to keep myself in check right now, I stay as still as possible, holding my breath. If I attempt to move, even to leave, I may not have enough control to keep me from lunging at Chris and the delicious offering he has pooling in his palm right now.

I feel my blood as it begins to pump through my veins at the sight of the crimson liquid. My heartbeat thunders in my ears and my breathing becoming erratic as the first wave of hunger floods my system. My skin flushing at the heat that is building inside of me at the blood lust and the memory of its taste.

The first time I consumed blood was when I turned and bit Adira, but it wasn't my only time. One time, I had nicked my finger and popped it in my mouth like any other time to help stop the bleeding. Only I found myself savouring it and sucking harder to draw out as much of the substance as possible.

The next time it happened was during a treatment at the clinic, there was a small amount left in a blood bag after my transfusion. I'm not proud of it, but when everyone was gone I had emptied what little was left into a cup and finished it. My body relished in it both times it happened, and I got the same energy burst, and both times I ended up craving it a little more afterwards.

"Luce?" Chris's masculine voice breaks through my mental haze. I shake my head vehemently, hoping to get him to stop talking because the silk sound his voice is projecting is causing a purr deep within me, and I'm help-less to its pull.

I take an involuntary step forward, my eyes

completely enthralled by the gash on his hand dripping droplets of life onto the counter. I know how wrong it is, but I want nothing more than to climb atop the marble surface and lick it up like a starved cat lapping up milk for the first time.

"What's going on Luce?" Chris whispers taking a tentative step forward, his hands held up towards me in a placating manner. I track his every movement like a predator stalking its prey, unwilling to let him out of my sight. I can almost guarantee my eyes have taken on that brilliant yellow glow that the undead sport, but I can't focus enough to care.

It's taking every fibre of my being not to leap over this counter and wrap myself around his torso while I drink him in. So as long as he doesn't come any closer, I am pretty sure I can escape, with both of us unscathed.

I look up to determine my best route out and catch a glimpse of the open blood bag on his counter. My breath catches in my throat and a little more of my control slips, making me take a step to the left, closer to the space where Chris and the source of my desire occupy. Chris is staring at me, watching my every move with a ferocious intensity, as though trying to decipher some code.

"Lucie? Are you hungry?" His words, chosen carefully, slam into me like a mack truck and setting off warning bells all through my head.

Why would he ask me that?

And it's in that moment I realize he knows. Somehow, he knows exactly what is happening and what this current situation is doing to me. Frantic, I search the room for an exit, knowing I won't have govern over my body soon. As if reading my thoughts, Chris drops the towel that was wrapped around his self inflicted injury and steps to the right, blocking my exit from the kitchen.

"Please don't go. We need to talk about this Lucie," Chris pleads with me.

But I can't focus on anything but his wounded hand. He sliced his palm, a deep score right across the middle, leaking his essence onto the floor.

My body begins to tremble at the thought of it, and I have to close my eyes to regain a semblance of self control before something happens I can't take back. Because right now, I'm breaking fast and I don't know if I can stop myself.

Chris has moved closer to me without my awareness as I wage a war within myself, and when his soft voice is right in front of me, I start slightly.

"Do it." His voice like sex when he leans in and whispers right next to my ear.

A shiver rolls through my body at his words and a fire begins to build inside me at his closeness. Goosebumps spread across my skin as I inhale the masculine scent of campfire and leather that he carries, invading my senses completely. He steps in further, forcing me to step back and corners me into the counter, making sure I have nowhere to go.

"Do it little one," he says again and this time my resolve breaks completely. I snatch his hand up and bring it to my mouth. I look him directly in the eyes as I sweep my tongue across his outstretched palm and hum in approval at the taste.

Must pull away.

Chris's blood coats my teeth and gums, my body tingling at the sensation of having him inside me.

I want more. NEED more.

My fingers curl around his wrist pulling his arm closer as a haze clouds my vision and blood lust consumes me. I close my mouth tighter over the wound and try to take in long drags, but Chris flinches and I still instantly.

"Luce…" my name a hiss on his lips, lingers in the air.

What the fuck am I doing?

Panic and shame collide, and the force of what I've done makes me let go, stumbling backwards away from Chris.

"Lucie stop! We can talk—"

But I don't let him finish as embarrassment slams into me at what just transpired. I step further away, mortified at my behaviour and lack of control as the tears begin to fill my eyes and overflow onto my cheeks.

Before either of us can do something we'll regret, I take off towards the front door. Chris tries to stop me, but it's no use. I'm too fast for him now.

What the fuck is wrong with me? What if I turned him? How did I let this happen or let it get this far? No one knew this side of me, and now the one person I couldn't imagine knowing, does.

CHAPTER 11

CHRIS

Fuck!

Well that didn't go as planned. Don't get me wrong I was successful in finding out what I needed to know, but at what cost?

I already had a feeling that Lucie was craving blood and what it did to her. I didn't mean to push it that far, but I also wasn't expecting to feel the same high she did, from watching her lick it off the palm of my hand. When I watched her eyes dilate and lust take over, it took everything I had to fight my own body's instinct to not grab her hips and crush her body into mine. To feel her against me while she took what she needed to survive. But when she pulled away, I knew I had to let her.

As much as I didn't want her to go, I knew she couldn't stay either. Had she stayed any longer, there is no way I would be accountable for my actions. Even now, the want to go after her drums through my veins as the beat of my heart continues to pound wildly out of control.

The pain in my hand pulls me from my reverie and I know that before I can do anything else I need to take care of this cut. It wasn't my intention to cut so deep, and the throbbing is now beginning to become unbearable after being manipulated and lapped at. If I don't take care of it right away, I risk getting an infection, and since we don't have antibiotics at our constant disposal, something so simple as a small cut, can become a big problem.

At that exact moment, a thought pops into my head and I'm not sure why I haven't considered it before. Actually that's a lie, I know damn well why I never *wanted* to consider this before, but sometimes, you gotta make sacrifices for the ones we love.

This is such a bad idea. I knew it would be a hard sell, but I didn't expect this much of a fuss from Bea. If she would just get her head out of her ass and think about what I'm proposing, I know she would agree with me, but the old coot is stubborn to the core.

"He ain't coming with me. Simple as that." Bea crosses her arms like a sullen teenager while she glares at me.

"You were the one that said, *come out with me pretty boy*," I mock the witch's voice from the *Wizard of Oz* as I spew her own vile words back at her, waiting for her tantrum to end.

"Come on Bea, we need all the help we can get. And Chris is the only one willing to go with you. You and I both know we need this run more than most and it needs to happen soon. Our supplies are dwindling and fast," Lochlan practically begs her to see his reasoning.

After what feels like forever, Bea finally concedes and tosses her hands in the air.

"Fine! I'll take him with me, but I will not be held responsible if he mysteriously vanishes or I return one person light." She points to me and then at Lochlan to solidify her point. And with a curt nod, she turns on her heel and jumps in the passenger side of the truck, leaving me to drive.

Just as I'm about to go join Bea for the ride from hell, Lochlan whistles at me and flags me over to where he's stepped out of everyone else's earshot.

"Listen, I know we all get a kick out of the fact that Bea is always joking about killing you, but truthfully…" he glanced around and slings his arm around my shoulders pulling me in to his side. "I'm not one hundred percent convinced she's joking. Now I'm not saying she is going to try and kill you herself, but I also wouldn't necessarily count on her assistance in keeping you alive either. Keep your eyes and ears open. Watch your six, and come back safe and alive." He pats my back and sends me off to my death.

I may have over extended myself on this one.

Fuck this is gonna suck.

CHAPTER 12

CHRIS

Bea and I have been driving for hours, plowing our way through what's left of the snow and zombies as we make our way to our first stop. The streets barren, cars abandoned, and the snow covering it all like a clean white blanket preserving the life beneath it.

"Looks like nobody's been here in awhile," Bea says as she keeps her eyes open for any signs of life. Or lack thereof.

"What makes you say that?" Genuinely curious as to how she came to that conclusion.

"First, there's no tracks in the snow. New or old. Second, there is no signs of snow removal or vehicle traffic anywhere. Even without a plow or vehicle, you would still need to remove some of this snow to get around by foot." She whistles out through her teeth.

Well, shit. I never would have come to those conclusions within the few moments of driving through the deserted town streets. Her observations are clinical and precise but crucial. As the passenger, she needs to be on her A game and be the eyes of two people while the other navigates. Both responsible for each other as much as themselves.

At the realization of how vital Bea is to Lucie's survival, a new respect for Bea grows and I find myself hating her just a little bit less.

"Let's start with a grocery store. Small town, means smaller population. More supplies, less zombies to create and less for us to worry about or kill. We might have just hit the jackpot Romeo," Bea says with a hint of a smile. Or the closest thing resembling a smile she could conjure.

Pulling up to the grocery store, Bea directs me to go around the back to the loading bay. "It's easier to load the truck if you're level with it, as opposed to lifting in and out. We can do less trips faster and gather more product," Bea informs me at my questioning look from her instructions. I hate to say it, but the old broad is pretty good at this and I get why she's so successful out here.

"Park there and turn off the engine. Leave the key in the ignition. I have a spare on me and there is another spare in the wheel well in a neon green case if needed." I nod at her instructions and make a mental note of where everything is, if shit hits the fan.

Bea jumps out and grabs her personal arsenal from where she stashed it and I follow suit. She easily pops the door open and steps inside searching for the gate chain to open the loading bay door. When she finds it and starts to pull, the metal screeching sound echoes throughout the building. We pause waiting to hear if there is anyone or anything still inside making its way to us.

After a few minutes of silence, Bea shrugs and

continues to open the large door and allowing light to spill through. I stand and watch for anything moving in the shadows, ready to remove any threats but it seems we're alone. For now.

We get everything organized and grab large warehouse carts ready to be filled. We roam aisle to aisle collecting a bit of everything, making sure to have as much variety as possible. We ensure we have the necessities and even grab a few indulgent items for ourselves. Perks of the job according to Bea.

As I munch down on my bag of stale Doritos and enjoy my treat, still stacking multiple items on my over-flowing cart, I hear an odd sound from the next aisle over. The aisle I know Bea is currently occupying.

"Bea?" I whisper shout, unsure of what or who could be accompanying us. But I'm only greeted with silence. When the sound of a thud hitting concrete reaches my ears, I don't think and run to the source of the noise.

There on the ground is Bea, lying lifeless in a fragile looking heap in the middle of the grocery aisle.

No, no, no, no. This can't be happening.

Fuck!

Shit!

I gather Bea's limp body into my arms and take off at a dead run towards the truck. I don't bother to grab anything or close up the building as I gently deposit Bea onto the floor in the back, wrapping her in whatever I can reach.

"Hang on, Bea, I got you."

Absolutely frantic, I spin out of the parking lot and

fish tail down the road not even caring what ruckus we create, hell bent on making it back to the compound before it's too late.

Please don't die.

I practically plow through the front gates of the compound, never slowing and weaving my way through the narrow streets to the clinic. I'm blaring my horn to get everyone to move, but all it does is draw attention to us, not make the trip faster.

Finally reaching the clinic on the opposite end of the compound, I slam on the brakes and slide right past the fucking door as my truck and trailer struggles to halt its forward momentum at this speed. When I manage to come to a complete stop, I jump out and rush around to grab Bea.

Crashing through the front doors and taking everyone off guard, I hear a few shrieks of astonishment. I don't bother to apologize, because frankly, I don't care.

"Get Dr. Tanner!" I shout at anyone who will listen to me as I take Bea to the closest bed and deposit her for examination.

"What happened?" Dr. Tanner asks, clinical mode firmly in place as she begins taking vitals and assessing Bea.

"I have no idea. She collapsed while we were out on a run and been like this since. She's breathing, that's all I know." I lift my hands in surrender and step back letting Dr. T get to work.

"How long has she been like this?" Dr. Tanner asks but never looks away from Bea as she lies lifeless on the bed.

"I- I don't know, almost two hours now." I fill her in on what little details I have, but it's not much and none of it will be of any assistance.

I fist my short locks and begin to pace as a restless energy settles in at the thought of having to tell Lucie. She and I aren't on good terms as it is, and now this?

Fuck she's gonna hate me.

CHAPTER 13

Lucie

The moment I open the door, the scent of campfire and leather assault me and instantly the bloodlust returns. My body recognizing his scent, my mouth begins to salivate and my stomach growls at the promise of nourishment.

My cheeks flush pink as embarrassment washes over me at the memory of last night and I duck my head to try and conceal it from him. The last thing I need is to give Chris another reason to harass me about something that I find mortifying.

"Lucie, can I come in?" Chris's voice is so low I can barely hear him. He called me Lucie. Not Luce or little one, but Lucie. I look up into his eyes, desperately trying to find something that will let me in on his secret, but I come up empty handed, his expression unreadable.

Unease washes over me so powerful that I stumble backwards into the house, prompting Chris to follow my retreat, ready to catch my tumbling form.

Something isn't right, I can feel it. Something bad.

Chris doesn't say anything, just stares into my eyes as

his face gentles by the second, solidifying what I suspected.

Bea.

My body crumbles beneath me and I slide down the wall, no longer able to hold my weight as the reality of Chris's silence settles over me. Chris crouches down and cradles me into his chest. I grip his arms and sob into his shirt, thinking the absolute worst has happened.

"Is she…" I can't force out the words and I almost gag trying to swallow them back down. Bea has been the only adult in my life that wasn't paid to be part of it. She's the closest thing to family I've ever known and the thought of not having her here breaks something within me.

"No, but she's not well." His words give me hope, as his voice caresses my skin and leaves a tingle in its wake. I know I shouldn't enjoy being in his arms, taking advantage of his kindness, but I don't have the strength to pull away.

Sadness overwhelms me at the thought of Bea leaving me to face what's left of this world alone and at the same time, I almost hate her for it. She took me in, fed me, cared for me, made me need her for the last four years, and now she wants to fucking leave me? I won't let her. I refuse to let her go.

A new wave of despair crashes through me at my clusterfuck of emotions being at war with themselves, causing frustration to build and adding another to the pile helping to drain to my already depleting energy source.

Fatigue begins to battle me for dominance at my overactive mood swings and can tell my body is going into overdrive as tremors develop in my limbs. My stomach begins to growl, and my eyes begin to glow, a telltale sign the virus is actively coursing through my system and demanding to be sated.

My eyes practically their own light source at this point, letting me know I am on the brink of my precipice. Exhausted by the whirlwind inside of me, I try to conjure the last bit of strength I possess to push myself away and to my feet, but I can barely lift my head from Chris's shoulder, let alone support my entire body.

Another hunger pain grips me and this time I fold into myself as the unbearable need to feed bears down on me.

Chris shifts beneath me and relief settles my restlessness momentarily, knowing he will be taking me to the hospital to get a transfusion.

Except that's not what happens at all.

"Luce, you need to feed." He says it so casually and matter of fact that I almost believe there is nothing fucked up about the fact that I need blood of some sort in order to survive and that he is offering it.

Chris reaches behind his back and produces a small blade and pops it open. He lifts it to his wrist and I struggle against him to pull away from the temptation he's offering, but I can barely lift my hand two inches.

"Lucie, you can barely open your eyes. You need your strength to be strong for Bea." His tone harsh, like a father demanding reason from a child.

I know he's right ,but I can't bring myself to do it. How can he offer something like this? How is he not turned off or disgusted by it? By me?

Thump thump.

Chris's heartbeat pounds against my ear and locks my attention. Enthralled by the blood that flows just below the surface of Chris's skin, tempting me as I watch his vein throb with life. I remember what it was like, flowing down my throat. I don't *just* remember it. I want it. *Crave* it. And I'm not sure how long I can hold off, my inner-demon fighting its way to the surface, clawing for freedom.

I'm not so sure I want to fight it anymore. Chris's blood calls to me, tempting me in ways I can't ignore. The closer he gets to me, the more I slip and the more my hunger grows. My stomach growls, screaming in demand as his alluring scent envelops me.

"Do it, little one." Chris's voice slithers into my subconscious and breaks the small hold I had on my demon.

"What if I make you turn?" my voice so soft, I'm not even sure he heard me.

"You won't. Adira can't." He answers so sure that I won't be his harbinger of death.

"I'm not Adira. My case is different. You of all people should know that." I nod to our current situation for emphasis.

"I'm pretty sure if I was going to turn, I already would have," Chris says, putting his head down, probably a little turned off at his admission.

No longer able to resist, I nod in surrender and Chris shuffles me so I'm straddling his waist, supporting my weight and head on his chest. The next thing I know,

Chris is pulling my head back and offering me his wrist that is overflowing with life.

I latch on, and this time I make an effort to slow down and not cause him pain like last time. I take small tentative pulls, not wanting to seem greedy, but when Chris's other hand cups the back of my head and he moans in approval, everything changes. The intoxicating feeling of arousal accompanies each drop blood that passes over my lips as an inferno of lust breaks free from deep within.

In a snap, the bloodlust takes over and I grind down on his thigh as my body undulates against him involuntarily. Chris's hand fastens onto my hip as he makes a sound that resonates in his chest, and I pull him incredibly closer, breathing him in and growling back in response.

I take another pull from his wrist and my hips match the movement, rocking against him. He thrusts his hips up into me at the same time as he pulls me down, and I can feel him growing harder beneath his jeans. He's getting off on this just as much as I am, and that only seems to fuel my desire further.

I pull away from his wrist and turn towards him, my bloodlust giving me a confidence I've never had before, and press my lips to his. He stills in my arms, hesitating for only a second, before he takes control of the kiss with a brutal attack.

His tongue darts out, sweeping across my lower lip, begging for entrance, and I don't deny him. I open and let him take what he wants, because it's what I want too. What I've always wanted but could never have.

It's always been, "Lucie, you're like my little sister"

or "You're too young to know or understand." All bullshit answers that mean nothing right now. Because right now, I know they were all lies. He wants this just as bad as I do, if not more.

I wrap my arms around his neck ready to take things a little further when, suddenly, Chris pulls back, gripping my arms to hold me in place and keeping me just out of reach as he catches his breath.

"We have to stop." His whispers, as he leans his forehead against mine. "They're waiting for us at the clinic."

His words feel like a bucket of ice water poured over my head bringing me back to reality and the reason he showed up here in the first place. How could I forget about Bea? She's in the hospital hurt, *or worse*, and I'm over here getting my jollies off with her nemesis.

What the fuck is wrong with me?

I pry myself from his embrace and move to the opposite wall of the entryway, trying to put as much distance between us as possible while I gather my now growing strength. Clearly, I have zero control when it comes to Chris and the last couple of days just proves it.

Chris stands and holds his hand out to me, but I don't take it or even bother to acknowledge it or him. Instead, I focus on getting myself under control and being there for Bea.

Frowning at my dismissal, Chris grabs my coat and wraps it around me, leading me out the door towards the clinic. He doesn't know that the cold doesn't bother me anymore and I'm not about to tell him. He already knows too much.

Shame once again washes over me at the events that have transpired and the sting of being rejected twice by Chris in just as many days is sobering. I can't believe I did that. *Again.* This time I practically humped his leg like a dog in heat.

Fuck!

We're lucky he was able to pull away, because the same couldn't be said for myself. He stopped things before they went too far and both of us regretted it. Although, based on his look of shame, I don't think I would have regretted it as much as he would have.

I try to shake that thought, but the only thing more powerful than the shame of rejection twice is remembering what he felt like under me when I took control. The feel of his hard length pressed tight against my heated core as I writhed on his lap.

Shit, this is gonna be harder than I thought.

CHAPTER 14

CHRIS

I slept like shit last night after what happened between Lucie and I, making my mood foul as fuck. It doesn't help that being in the god damned zombie apocalypse means no fucking coffee either.

I'm also getting sick and tired of all these impromptu meetings that all seem to be mandatory and always when I'm having a shit day.

"I don't know what's wrong with her. I can't tell for sure without doing imaging and running blood work, but I suspect liver failure or cancer. And we just don't have the equipment here to confirm the diagnosis either way," Dr. Tanner informs us somberly.

Lochlan, Dante, Tripp, Grey, Adira and myself all sit around the table as Dr. T informs us, yet again, that we need more supplies. Supplies that no one is able to get, except the two people unable to get them.

"What about taking Bea to the equipment? Do the tests there in the hospital, then get out?" Dante asks. His question is valid, but not possible.

"We can't take the risk of moving her. Also, we don't

know if there is power in these places to run the equipment long enough," Dr. Tanner answers him, but that is not the reason we can't do it, that's the reasons we shouldn't.

"Hospitals are the worst places to go now. Everyone needs something from there and those that don't are just looking for drugs. There's no way you would have the time to pull something like that off," Adira adds on.

"Then how the fuck have they been doing it all this time?" I throw my hands up exasperated. "Lucie's never told me it was that bad, and her and Bea—"

"I told her not to," Lochlan cuts me off, dropping his gaze to the table.

"Not to what?" I ask cautiously, not sure where he's going with this. And based on his heavy sigh and how his demeanor changes instantly, I'm not sure I'm gonna like it.

"I told them not to tell anyone what it was really like going out there doing all these runs. I didn't have them down play it enough that everyone wanted to do it, but enough no one put up a fuss about it either," Lochlan says as he begins to pace the floor.

"And they agreed to this bullshit?!" I practically screamed at him. Why the fuck would they agree to it all if it's that dangerous? But I already knew the answer to that question. Bea goes for Lucie and Lucie goes for everyone else. Lucie wants to feel wanted. She needs it and doing these runs gives her that.

"What about Adira?" I ask. "She's the strongest person we got, I'm sure that if anyone can do this run, she could."

"I need her here. Her blood is everything right now, so I need to keep her alive to ensure others survive. I can stop the change with her blood at the right moment, but it must be fresh blood," Dr. Tanner advises us of her current work. "There's something else." She leaves her words hanging heavy in the air.

"What is it Doc?" Lochlan grits through his teeth, knowing full well that this is not going to be good news.

"We, uh, we need more blood. Lucie has been going through it faster and people in the community are not as generous with giving theirs…" Her voice trails off as her words sink in.

"Fuck!" I shout and ram my fist into the nearest wall.

Here we go again.

CHAPTER 15

Lucie

C hris left.
He just up and fucking left without saying a word.

Again.

I had to find out from Dr. Tanner this morning when she popped in to check on Bea that he and a crew went on a hospital run. I haven't left Bea's side since she was admitted almost two days ago and slept here last night, not able to go back to our house. I didn't want to look at her empty chair and I didn't want the ol' bat to wake up alone. She's been alone her whole life, other than Joe of course, but she isn't going to die that way.

However, the moment I found out that Chris had gone out with a small group of guys to get the equipment needed to determine what was wrong with Bea, I ran home and grabbed a walkie talkie that I picked up on a recent haul. It allows me to listen in on the channel these guys use and anyone around us. I have it low so that I can take in everything they're saying. But right now, until they are back within range, all I hear is the nonsense chatter of the guys working the fence and static.

As constant worry and fear begin to take its toll on my body, I decide to lay my head down and preserve my strength.

Movement from under my hand jolts me awake and I snap to attention. There sits Bea, propped up against the hospital bed, sporting a miserable look while taking in her surroundings. When her eyes lock on mine, her face softens and her fingers reach out to me.

"Hey girl, you alright? Your eyes are looking a little pale," she says sadly. I know this whole thing with me being a hybrid has her worried and she feels responsible for me, but I hate seeing her look at me like that.

"Hey lady." I can barely choke out as emotion floods me and I jump from my chair into her outstretched arms. I don't bother to fight the tears as she rocks me back and forth on her hospital bed. She's the one sick, yet she still takes care of me.

"What happened?" I manage to get out between snif-fles and snorts. This is the first time in almost 48 hours that she's opened her eyes and this is the first time in the four years that we've known each other that she has ever hugged me.

"I'm old. It was bound to happen eventually. Don't worry your pretty little self about me girl. Now, before my meds can kick in again, grab my bag from over there." She points to the opposite side of the room. Barely.

I do ask she asks and grab her bag bringing it back and sitting next to her on the bed. I open the zipper for her and just as I'm about to dump the contents, the alarm on my walkie talkie goes off.

"There's a herd on our ass, and our vehicle is severely damaged. Sprinters. A lot of fucking sprinters. I don't think we're gonna make it." I hear Chris's voice come over the radio and instantly I'm alert.

The sound of fear in Chris's tone spurs me into action at the thought of how much danger he's in right now. There is no way we have enough firepower to take out a herd before they reach the gate. It would just be too close and would put the whole community at risk if one were to get in.

They need a distraction. Something to pull the zombie's attention from the boys coming in while the gate is open and I have just the thing. I look to Bea for permission to head out and she gives a slight nod.

"I hate to say this, but you're gonna have to go save that boy's ass," Bea says making a face as though the words themselves tasted like vinegar to say. I chuckle and kiss her forehead before heading out of the clinic, making sure to let Heidi know she's awake before dashing down the street to where I have my truck parked. I haven't needed to use this one yet, but am excited to.

I jump in the old fashioned tow truck and hook my megaphone up to the roof and head out. I scroll through my playlist, searching for the loudest, attention grabbing song I can find.

I pull up to the gates, revving my engine obnoxiously, waiting to be unleashed as everyone stares at me in horror.

I have spent the last three months cooped up in this place, depressed at the fact that my life is no longer my own, constantly at the mercy of my cravings and being told I'm a liability. Being told what to do, where to go and where I'm not allowed. But that stops now.

I am capable of just about anything. My limitations, almost non existent. I feel stronger than I have since I was bitten and I plan to take full advantage of that. Time to finally see what I'm made of. Adira has all these extra abilities, and I too have discovered some amped up skills I've acquired with her help.

Excitement builds at the thought of my untapped potential and I feel almost giddy with adrenaline. I feel the power begin to rush through my veins and the endorphins kick in as I take a deep steadying breath.

Lochlan stares at me through the front windshield and it's not in curiosity or concern. He's merely determining that I'm the only one he's willing to sacrifice at this moment due to my current situation. And right now, I'm his best option to ensure the highest rate of survival and he knows it. Whether I live or die, he's ok with either outcome as long as the community is safe.

Lochlan, still staring, trying to find a weakness or hesitation but he won't find one and when he realizes it, he nods and gestures to open the gate.

Hearing Chris's engine getting louder, clearly struggling and seeing the smoke billowing from the hood, as his tuck is pushed beyond its limits, I crank the loud speaker with a song guaranteed to get the attention of the sprinters, praying to keep them away from him and the open gate.

The moment I have enough room, I race through the narrow opening, barely keeping both side mirrors as Adira jumps on my truck. I push open the door as she slides in with ease, holding my stare for only a brief moment, enough to make sure I got this, then nods to let me know she has my back.

We fist pump knowing we can make a huge dent in this population of z's and since we already know how each other fight, having been working together for months without anyone's knowledge, we have the advantage.

But it's gonna be one hell of a shock for everyone else. Especially Lochlan. No one wanted me out on the runs, or to learn how to defend myself or use my strength, because I'm unpredictable, a question mark.

"Why train someone who could turn on you and use it against you?" I believe were Lochlan's exact words in a meeting I eavesdropped on. But this is my chance for me to prove to everyone that I am not broken or fragile like they've been treating me. Or that I'm gonna turn into a monster or turn on them. That I'm still the same person and can do all the things I could before, only better.

At that realization, I speed up knowing Lochaln is gonna chase Adira and I to try and stop us from going out there, and I see Adira smile at me when she realizes.

We got this.

"No one shoots once that truck hits the field. Fucking no one!" Lochlan screams over the radio.

"Lochlan, NO!" Chris shouts back as we cross paths his eyes locked on mine.

"Adira!" Lochlan tries again, but she just leans over and turns off the radio and focuses on our task at hand.

Here we go.

I drop the plow at the front and turn on my wipers as I hit the first of the group, spray painting everything red and black. I pull the handbrake and spin my ass end out taking out more of the group, while tramping them under my oversized mud tires.

"Hang on," I tell Adira as I flip a switch and the tow chain drops as I let out its entire length.

I take a second to line it up and then gun it. Adira reaches up, grabbing the "oh shit" handle as I swing the truck around, yanking my backend out to snap the chain like a whip.

The hook from the tow truck, now airborne, slices through the mass of bodies removing heads and torsos as I pull the chain tight by speeding up. A couple more loops and passes, we have 90% of the herd taken care of.

I maneuver the truck through the field of dismembered bodies to finish off the last of them, some still crawling on the ground, using their arms to drag them forward, when I feel the truck get stuck in the thawing ground.

I know we're going to have to fight our way back to the gate or at least see if we can free the truck, but either way, we're gonna end up facing off the horde of teeth. At the thought of being outside the confines of the vehicle and away from the safety it provided, I suddenly remembered what it's like to have those teeth embedded in my flesh. Flashbacks of Joe, the attack at the clinic, being bitten and the pain following it, all flood my vision and I begin to tremble.

Adira must see my panic because she leans over and grabs my hand, giving it a tight squeeze as she looks me dead in the eyes and whispers, "You got this. You're stronger than they are. Faster. You're the predator now."

Her words slam into me, and determination takes over and I know it's time to test the limits of the strength I possess. Training with Adira has been great, but we've been practicing with each other, not going full tilt and excitement begins to bubble over at the thought of letting go of my reservations and seeing what I can really do. We've all seen what Adira can do, but like I've said before, we're not the same.

I leave the music blaring to keep the infected's attention away from the gate while they try and push Chris's vehicle across the threshold, but that means we have all that unwanted attention on us.

Grabbing my bat, I use the truck door to launch myself from the cab, swinging at the closest target. With my new strength it only takes one hit to eliminate the threat, as the metal chain wrapped around the top half of my bat makes contact, spraying blood and pieces of fractured skull in every direction.

I feel the force of the hit radiate up my arms, but instead of feeling pain or fatigue like I expected, I get the exact opposite. Endorphins flood my bloodstream and I become almost feral with the amount of power coursing through my veins.

I bring the bat up, slicing it through the air with a strength I didn't know I possessed, and the Z's skull collapses on itself from the force of the blow and the fear of being bitten, all but forgotten. I can feel the vibrations in the ground as another one comes up beside me, but before he even gets within biting distance, I've sent what's left of its head rolling in the now blood covered field.

Lochlan won't have to worry about newcomers anymore, based on the horror movie display we've just created. I'm betting this will turn away anyone looking for refuge now.

I can hear the angry shouts at the gate, and the sounds of Adira still fighting on her side of the truck, so I take advantage and try to see if I can get the truck unstuck. My side doesn't seem that bad, but when I make my way around the back, I notice the entire rear passenger tire is sunk right up to the metal frame of the truck. There is no chance in hell I'm getting this thing out quickly or without a little effort and some tools.

Adira walks over ready to aid me, when I hear something run up behind us. Twisting out of the way I reach up to grasp its head in an attempt to remove it, but my fingers imbed into its skull right next to another set. I look up, locking eyes with Adira's glowing pupils, almost positive they mirror my own, and without a word, we pull in opposite directions, feeling the skin and bones begin to separate then break, as the last Z's body comes apart in two pieces.

Warm blood and debris litter our skin and clothing, and I have to fight the urge not to gag at the smell of the dead undead. The stench so thick I can almost chew it. Adira takes a step forward prepared to soothe me, but it's not necessary. I wave off her concern and she smiles in return, respect written on her face at how well I'm taking it. This should bother me, and I should be grossed out, but the only thing that really bothers me about all this... is that it really doesn't bother me at all.

Adira and I make our way back to the gates and am shocked at the fact that I'm not unconscious after using so much energy on the field, given my history as of late. But maybe Chris is onto something with this whole feeding thing. Each time I've ingested blood directly the longer my strength seems to last.

Maybe that's the key. Not swap the blood out, but drink it instead?

Fuck that sounds crazy. I'm not a vampire for fuck sakes.

Or am I?

To be honest, I don't know what's possible anymore. I mean look around, we're in the fucking zombie apocalypse, I won't rule out anything at this point. No matter how crazy that makes me sound.

I contemplate the possibilities of what this means but the moment we breach the gate threshold, we're bombarded by both Lochlan and Chris and a shit ton of questions.

"What the fuck was that?" Chris demands, but I know he's not looking for an actual answer and he isn't going to get one either. I don't know if it's the adrenalin from what went down, or the virus itself altering my personality, but I feel different, and this time he won't be talking to me like some insolent child.

"What the fuck was what? Me saving your ass?" I shoot back not even bothering to give him my eyes as my annoyance laces each word. His eyes go wide in shock at my tone, having never heard it towards him before, but too fucking bad.

Quickly schooling his features, his face retreats to the same angry look as before when he stomps towards me. "Are you fucking kidding me right now? You know better than to go out there, you could have gotten yourself killed! And where the fuck did you learn to fight like that?" His voice so loud it's practically a squeak by the time he finishes his sentence.

"I'm not doing this with you. I'm sick and tired of doing *this* with you." I point back and forth between us. "If you have an issue with the fact that I went out there, take it up with Lochlan. He was the one who opened the gate. Otherwise, suck. It. The. Fuck. Up." And with that, I turn my back to him while he absorbs my words and strip off my now blood soaked jacket.

I can hear a similar conversation being exchanged between Lochlan and Adira not more than ten feet away and I can't help the chuckle that escapes me as Adira looks over rolling her eyes at their reactions.

After listening to both Chris and Lochlan shout about

how reckless we were, I make my way back to the hospital to check on Bea and let her know I'm ok.

However, the moment I step inside her room, she kicks me out stating the stench of the undead is too much for her weak stomach to handle. I think she's going through detox and is just being miserable, but I can't be sure.

I leave Bea to go clean up, passing Chris on my way out of the clinic, completely ignoring him as he calls my name. He needs to realize I'm not a fucking child and that he can't tell me what to do and that his outburst is not acceptable or appreciated.

"Lucie, wait!" I hear him shout once more. Without turning around, I throw my middle finger in the air letting him know I'm not dealing with his shit anymore and can hear when everyone else laughs at my response. I hear him curse, but I no longer care. He treats me like a child, yet he's the one who acts like it.

I'm done being told what to do and sitting on the side-lines while everyone suffers.

CHAPTER 16

CHRIS

Dante's laughter rings through my ears as Lucie walks away from me, taking all the air from my lungs with her. I don't think of the consequences as I cock my hand back and let it fly connecting hard with his jaw and knocking him off his feet.

"What the fuck?!" D screams.

"Chris!" Grey and Lochlan shout at the same time but I'm already walking away and heading toward my house.

Fuck them. D's always talking shit, and today he pushed too far.

I storm through the front door, sending it crashing into the drywall behind it. But I don't stop there. I tear my jacket off, launching it down the hallway and taking out a lamp on the entryway table as I make my way into the kitchen, searching for something to drink.

Lucie walked away. Lucie *fucking* walked away. From me!

My chest tightens at the thought of Lucie not wanting to be near me and I reach up to massage the ache that's left behind in her absence. I know I yelled at her, but watching her out there, unprotected, fighting like that made me feel physically sick to my stomach.

"Fuck!"

I swipe my hand across the counter and knock everything onto the floor with a loud crash as pieces of broken glass and cutlery scatter across its surface.

I reach under the sink and grab the bottle of rye I had hidden for a day such as this, removing the cap and taking a long swig, savoring the feeling as it burns the entire way down, followed by a few more.

After a few more drinks, my thoughts become chaotic and the desperate need to be near Lucie overwhelms me. I know she won't want to see me, she made that very clear, but I can't stay away. I need the calm only she can gift me. I need to be near her, any part of her.

A thought slams into my head and I'm out the door in the next instant, making my way back towards the clinic, bottle still in hand.

I pass the "nurses station" and head right for her room, tapping on the door. Bea's pale grey eyes meet mine in surprise before they lock on my hand currently holding the bottle of rye.

"What are you doing here boy? " she asks, her voice sounding more hoarse than normal. I hold up the bottle and pray she won't turn me away. I'm not sure my psyche can handle the rejection twice.

"Pull up a chair," she says while pulling herself into a sitting position and letting loose a cough so vile sounding I feel it in my own bones. A sharp pang of guilt wracks my entire body as I listen to the reason we needed those machines. I would offer her help, but I know better than to offend Bea like that.

Instead, I grab her cup and empty the water in the sink, replacing it with my contraband and handing it to her. She looks from the cup to me and then taps it against my bottle to cheers and tosses it back, motioning for another.

I refill her cup and take a seat next to her bed as we watch old episodes of *Friends* on TV in silence until she passes out, leaving me to wade through my tempestuous thoughts.

CHAPTER 17

Lucie

I get dressed and head out early, having had no sleep and make my way to the garage, knowing Chris's truck will be there needing to be cleaned. Since I've been forced to stay behind these past three months, I've been helping out the mechanics to keep myself busy when I'm not with Adira. Nothing too crazy, but of course I get the dirty jobs, and today will be no exception.

I stepped into the shop ready to tackle my task at hand and get straight to work. I slowly walk the perimeter of the vehicle, trying to determine where to even begin. Mud, grass and gore coat the entire vehicle top to bottom and I dread the thought of what mine is going to look like if I can get it unstuck without being attacked.

This is gonna take me fucking hours.

I quickly spray everything down, removing the worst of the mess before doing a more thorough clean so that the boys can get a better look at the damage, when I see Chris standing in the doorway, his hair disheveled and hands in his pockets. Heavy dark circles shadow his eyes, clearly having not slept either.

We stare at each other for a moment, neither of us saying a word, before he breaks away and takes a seat in the corner. So much has changed between us, and a lot has happened in a very short period of time and I feel there's no coming back from it at this point.

Our relationship is no longer platonic, but it's not sexual, either. We straddle that line on the best of days, but now with this new added element, we're sitting in uncharted territory having no idea where to go from here. I have no idea how to even approach him at this point and fear this might be the end of our beginning.

I continue working, his eyes never leaving me for a second, but his silence is deafening and eating away at me slowly. The tension in the air builds, becoming almost palpable and I break the silence, unable to stand it anymore.

"What happened to the trailer?" I ask, genuinely curious.

"On the way back we ran into that group of sprinters. I thought I could just bust through them, but I didn't consider the trailer." His words begin to stumble out as he relives the nightmare of failing on a run. Something I know all too much about.

"The tire blew and it began to pull us like a slingshot as it weaved behind the truck out of control. The added weight from the machines caused it to flip and detach from our truck. The last I saw, it was rolling through the trees as pieces of metal flew everywhere." His eyes have glazed over at his retelling and the look of sorrow and guilt flash across his features. He runs his hands through his hair in frustration at the whole situation, knowing that someone now has to try and do what his team couldn't. He sighs and hangs his head into his hands, defeat heavy on his shoulders.

He goes quiet again after that and I let him. I feel like he needs this moment to just process everything that went down for him out there and for us in here. It's not easy doing these runs and putting yourself at risk, and of all people, I understand that more than most. I've had more close calls and holy shit moments than I care to admit.

I leave Chris to his silence and begin to wander around the vehicle, pulling away limbs and clumps of things I choose not to examine too closely. The smell begins to overwhelm me and I have to pull my bandana across my face to help block out some of the vile stench as I continue my assessment.

I bend over to get a better look underneath the vehicle, and hear Chris's intake of breath. Seconds later, I see Chris's boots come into view and I pause what I'm doing, waiting for him to speak. When he says nothing I lift my head to look at him, and he takes another step forward, forcing me to stand upright. I stumble back a bit unprepared at his invasion and his strong hands clamp down on my upper arms, keeping me steady and upright before falling on my ass.

I lift my head to glare at him, but my eyes widen when he steps into me, erasing the last few inches separating us. My heart thunders behind my ribs so loud I'm almost positive he can hear it, but I don't move a muscle. I try to swallow but it turns into an audible gulp.

Licking my now dehydrated lips, his eyes track the movement like a predator tracking its prey. His one hand leaves my shoulder, slowly sliding up my neck to my jaw, tilting my head back so he can look directly in my eyes. I can see the anguish clearly written on his face, but also hunger and lust as it wars for control. His eyes blaze with the potency of his desire and I watch the moment it wins out over the rest.

A deep blush creeps up my cheeks at the heat in his eyes, his lips so close to mine I can practically taste his breath on my tongue, and I'm almost positive I've stopped breathing. I start to squirm under his stare, unable to control my body's need to rub up against him like a cat in heat.

A smirk plays at his lips when he realizes my internal struggle and leans in to whisper in my ear. "When is your birthday Lucie?" His voice so low and gravelly as it skates across my skin, leaving goosebumps in its wake. I fight the moan currently threatening to escape from my throat but lose the battle when his head dips further into me, running his nose along the shell of my ear.

I'm pretty sure I just swallowed my fucking tongue.

"Tell me, little one." He tries again, but my head swims from his proximity and all coherent thoughts are gone.

I think a squeak comes out, but I really can't be sure.

"Tell me, because I am not sure how much longer I can wait," he says with a dangerous edge to his voice. Thrusting his hips forward, my body instantly heats at the contact, and sparks ignite everywhere we're connected.

His breath fans across my face and neck and I shiver from head to toe, forcing a whimper from my throat. My thighs rub together, chasing a friction to help ease the ache that's building just from being this close to him. He's barely even touched me for Christ's sake and already I know I'm soaked.

"Luce…." He lets my name linger in the air, a threat weaving into each letter, bringing me back to reality as it registers he asked me a question.

"I-I don't know," I answer honestly. Not quite sure why that even matters right now. My birthday is the last thing on my mind, believe me.

"Luce…" Chris growls and his eyes come down to gaze into my own as he rests his forehead against mine. "Don't play. I can't handle this right now. I need a fucking answer." He grinds his teeth as his hold on me tightens, clearly fighting for control.

"I don't know my exact birthday. I never celebrated it and no one ever brought it up in the foster homes, so neither did I. I've always just gone by the first of the year." I say pulling away ever so slightly, agitated that he's bringing this up right now.

He pulls away, and stares at me, his face like stone and completely unreadable. In the next instant, I watch as his pupils dilate and devour the white and ocean blue irises when the war he's raging breaks from its confines and consumes him whole.

Without so much as a warning, he has me thrown over his shoulder and is stomping out the back door of the shop. A squeal escapes my lips as the cold breeze caresses my skin from the early spring chill, but he doesn't stop or slow down.

I moan when I feel his hand reach up and cup my ass through my thin tights, giving it a squeeze. I try to wriggle free from his grasp when I see people staring at us, but it's no use.

He storms through his front door and up the stairs to, what I'm assuming is his room and tosses me over his head as I land on a plush surface.

"I've waited for what feels like forever, for this moment, little one."

CHAPTER 18

CHRIS

The moment my brain processes what she just said, I'm propelled into action, not even aware of my conscious decision to toss her over my shoulder caveman style and take off in the direction of my living quarters.

Her squeal covers me in goosebumps and I have to fight the moan that threatens to escape as I wonder if she sounds like that when she comes. I try to shake those thoughts until we make it back to my place, but it's no use. My hand snakes up and cups her plush ass to help steady her on my shoulder, but I can't help myself and give it a squeeze.

I pick up my pace because I am finding it hard not to throw her down on the closest surface and claim what's mine. But I've waited too long to be impatient now and I won't disappoint her. She deserves more than that.

I stalk through my front door, kicking it closed behind me as I take the stairs two at a time. I walk into my bedroom, and toss her onto the bed as she bounces on my mattress causing her tits to swell over the top of her shirt giving me a peek at what's to come. She squeaks in surprise and instantly blushes the moment she realizes we're in my room.

Fuck, I love that shade of pink.

I don't take my eyes off of her as she lays on my bed, creating a mental picture. Black thin tights hugged her toned legs as leather holsters lined both sides of her narrow hips and upper thighs, cradling a blade in each. Leather arm guards and shoulder pieces cover the exposed porcelain skin of her arms while a white tank top hangs loose across her chest.

I watch her breath hitch and she begins to squirm under my scrutiny. Her inexperience belies her earlier confidence and I can't help but smile as her bravado slips. I feel like a teenager ready to lose my virginity again with the way my body trembles in anticipation.

"Aren't you cold?" I ask as I run my hands up and down her legs, starting at the bottom and slowing inching my way up to the apex of her thighs. My dick jerks in my pants, knowing that I'm touching Lucie and I have to adjust myself to keep from becoming indecent in her presence.

"I, I-I don't feel the cold anymore." Her voice a mere whisper as she pants her response through stuttered breaths while watching my movements with a trained eye.

I don't stop my ministrations, pushing further and further up her thighs, until I finally reach the clasp to release her leather straps. My eyes never leave hers as I remove the blades and then release the holsters, first the left and then the right, dropping both to the floor. I reach down, running my finger along the seam where her tights meet her waist, easing it between the fabric and her skin. I groan at how soft she feels beneath my touch, making my cock throb between my legs.

I wrap my fingers around the fabric of her tights and pull gently. She lifts her hips to aid me in my quest, a flush spreading across her face and dipping lower to the top of her chest. Once her tights are gone, I break my stare with her and stand, glancing down, wanting to take her all in. I growl under my breath when I realize she wasn't wearing anything under her tights and a shudder rolls over me.

"Fuck," I groan, stroking myself through my jeans at the thought that she's been running around commando and wondering how many other times she's done it.

She's killing me. Literally fucking killing me.

I quickly pull my shirt over my head, tossing it off to the side along with my shoes, before making my way closer to her. Lucie crosses her arms, about to pull the hem of her shirt up, when I grab her wrists to halt her movements.

"Let me do it, little one." I lean in and purr my words in her ear as I inhale her lavender scent. I see the shiver, as it racks her body at my words, having the desired effect.

So responsive.

I grab the bottom of her tank top and slip it up and over her head slowly, tossing it to the floor where it joins the rest of our discarded items. I run my fingers down her arms and memorize the feel of her skin and the reactions she has when I touch her.

"Chris I-" I put my finger over her plump lips,

silencing her words. I don't want to give her the opportunity to say no. Don't get me wrong, I would never force myself on her, but I don't want her to talk herself out of it, either. I've waited too long for this moment to let either one of us, or anyone else ruin it.

I close the rest of the distance and replace my finger with my lips and press them against hers as I push her back down onto the mattress. She rises onto her elbows to watch as I step back and remove the rest of my clothes, all except my boxers.

I watch as Lucie drops her gaze from mine, unabashedly checking me out from head to toe, her eyes going wide at the obscene tent in my shorts as a salacious smile graces her face and I reciprocate the action, taking in my fill of what's about to be mine.

She's so soft and petite, having barely grown into her adult body. Her stomach flat as her hips flare slightly, giving me just enough to grab a hold of. Her breasts are perfectly round, the small dusty pink peaks becoming more pronounced under my stare. I reach out and run my thumb along the underside of her globes, up along the side and finally over the tip. Her breath hitches and I smile, savoring the sweet sound.

Fuck, she's gorgeous. I'm already right on the edge of control and everything about her is pushing me to my absolute limit, but the second the sound of my name falls from her pillow-like lips, that short leash snaps.

Swallowing the last bit of distance between us, I begin crawling up her body, pressing soft kisses to her skin as I go. I nip the tender flesh of the inside of her thigh before gently pushing her legs apart to fit myself between them.

"*Chris.*" She moans my name. Closing her eyes, she reaches down and laces her fingers in my hair, giving a gentle tug and I growl at the sting. I don't hesitate another second, leaning forward and dragging my tongue up her wet folds, humming in approval.

"Fuck, you taste incredible," I praise, worshipping her flavour on my tongue. She's everything I have ever imagined and dreamed of, only better. So much fucking better.

Lucie's back arches and I reach up with one hand, placing my palm on her stomach, pressing her gently back down onto the mattress. I leave my hand there and bring the other up to circle her opening before pressing a finger inside.

Lucie moans, and I increase my efforts trying to push her over the edge before I snap. Lucie's hips begin to rock against my face, her breathing becoming ragged between moans of pleasure as she removes one hand from my hair to tease her own nipple.

"Chris, fuck." She throws her head back in ecstasy as I add a second finger, never pulling my mouth away from her clit as I suck harder watching her squirm beneath me. Removing my hand from her stomach, I reach down to free my cock and give it a quick stroke, trying to ease the ache that's building inside from the sound of her moaning my name.

Lucie was moaning my fucking name.

"Chris... I think I'm going to ...oh god.." Lucie's words barely making sense as her climax hits. I curl my fingers upwards, and soon after she's falling over the edge and crying out. Her scream echoes off my bedroom walls and through the house, positive that if anyone were walking by they too could hear her.

That's right, let them hear you, little one.

I slow down my assault as she comes crashing back down to earth, her heavy breathing the only sound in the room. I crawl up her body, pressing my forehead to hers, taking a moment to stare into her eyes and accept the calm she brings me at having her in my arms. I inhale her scent and my hips thrust forward of their own accord, as it sparks a fire inside me.

I don't care about the consequences or what others will think anymore, she's mine. Always has been, always will be.

CHAPTER 19

Lucie

C hris crawls up my body at an achingly slow pace, tasting me as he climbs, making me very aware of the fact I'm naked in front of him. I thought I would be nervous or shy, but the reverent way he's looking at me sets all my worries at ease.

And when he presses his forehead to mine, I close my eyes and cherish this moment, never having expected it to happen. Don't get me wrong, I've thought of it multiple times, in multiple positions but never like this.

"Look at me, little one." He puts his finger under my chin, bringing my eyes back up to meet his, "This does not have to go any further if you don't want it to. You say the word and I'll stop," he whispers, but I can tell based on the look in his eyes and the way his dick is practically hulking out, that he doesn't want to stop. And neither do I.

"No, I don't want you to stop."

That seems to be all the confirmation he needs because next thing I know, Chris reaches up grabbing the headboard for leverage, refusing to take his other hand off of me and pulls his body upwards, thrusting deep, in one fluid motion. My eyes roll to the back of my head at the sensation and how full having him inside me feels.

"Look at me, Lucie. I need to see you." His voice strained. I do as he asks and gasp at the intensity shining back from his own eyes.

Each thrust shoves me further up the mattress until my head is braced against it, aiding in his assault. I put my hand up to push down further into him, needing to be closer still and feel him bottom out.

"God, I can't believe this is happening... So long…. So fucking long." His words taper off into grunts of satisfaction as his hips piston at a steady rhythm that brings me back to the brink of another orgasm.

"Fuck, Luce, I'm not gonna last."

Something about his words spurs me on, knowing that I'm the one turning him on and making him go crazy and the crack sounds through the air, as our mouths collide. My ability to be gentle is gone and I meet him thrust for thrust, chasing my pleasure.

A delicious friction in my core builds and I feel the first signs of bloodlust awaken. I try to reign it in but I'm too far gone at this point and have no chance in hell of holding back. My fingers, practically claws, tear down his back as I anchor myself to him and begin riding him from below.

"Shit," he hisses through his teeth drawing my attention to his mouth. His bottom lip plump and begging me to bite it. So I do. I lean up and take his lip between my teeth, sucking on it. I can feel his heartbeat through the veins in his lower lip and I growl, an animalistic sound.

"Your eyes." His words in awe shake me from the haze, but only slightly.

"Are you hungry, little one?" his voice a sensual sound that sends shocks of pleasure directly to my clit at its timbre.

"Mhmm," is all I can manage because the bloodlust is back and I'm a victim to its rule. I have no willpower as my body craves every single thing Chris is willing to give me. I want him inside me at the same time I take him inside me. I want to feel him lose control under me. Because of me. I want it all. Need it all.

He pulls away for only a second and reaches for something in the nightstand. A condom maybe? Instead he returns with a small pocket knife. He leans over me and makes a small incision on his shoulder, where it meets his throat.

My eyes zero in on the drops of blood bubbling to the surface with every pump of his heart, forcing out a drop each time. My mouth begins to salivate and my body becomes like a livewire, sparks of fire lighting me up from the inside out.

I lock eyes with Chris, and can see the yellow glow radiating on his face letting me know I'm in full virus mode. His nod of encouragement is my last straw of hope to restrain myself and I break.

Leaning up, I begin to slowly lick the crimson trail from his upper pec, to his collarbone, up to his shoulder and finally to the wound itself. I moan at his masculine flavour as its spice absorbs into my body and a cool balm replaces the fire currently burning out of control.

Without warning, my climax slams into me. My body shaking violently as the power of his blood, combined with the fierce orgasm sends me spiraling, desperately trying to find my footing but I'm too overwhelmed and I scream.

Not your sex kitten, pornstar or normal orgasm scream, I mean full on bloody murder scream. I lock up as Chris continues his brutal pace, chasing his own release and I almost black out.

Three more pumps and he throws his head back, letting loose a roar so loud I almost have to cover my ears from the sheer volume. He comes crashing down next to me as we both lay in silence trying to catch our breath, sweat dripping from both our bodies.

"Don't feed from anyone else, Luce." His words from out of nowhere, shock me.

"What?" I ask, not absolutely sure I heard him right.

"Don't feed from anyone else. This is a hard pass for me and something I think we should keep just between us. For now at least."

"Ok," is all I can manage before my eyes close without my permission and I'm lured into slumber, completely sated and spent.

CHAPTER 20

CHRIS

Sitting here in the council meeting is practically torture. All I can think about is going back to my place and spending the day in bed getting to know Lucie more intimately. I curse myself trying to think of anything but how fucking amazing she felt wrapped around me, to keep from getting hard, but it's no use.

She stayed with me last night, the first of many to come, and I don't think I slept a minute, fear of waking up and it all being a dream.

Nothing felt more right than having her in my bed. Her blond hair fanned across my pillow, wearing my shirt, covered in my blankets and wrapped in my arms. It should have always been like this. I know I'm nine years her senior and people frown upon that, but fuck, we are living in the god damned zombie apocalypse, there are more important things to worry about, like staying alive. I feel robbed of so much time we could have had together, angry at the faces staring at me right now, judging me for wanting her. But now that I have her, I won't be letting go. I don't care what anyone says, including Bea.

"I don't want to say this, but I think we should let Lucie go back on the road." Lochlan's words snap me from my fantasy at the sound of Lucie's name. I frown at the jealousy I feel just hearing her name on another man's tongue, even if it is Lochlan and he has his own woman.

"She doesn't have her heightened emotions under control yet and it takes a toll on her body every time she loses it. It could put the group at risk," Adira adds her thoughts to the matter.

"Thank god Chris's team was able to get me more blood bags on that last trip because I was getting pretty low. It's like her body feeds off the fresh blood cells and the virus burns them off so quickly and the nutrients are gone," Dr. Tanner offers her clinical opinion, although based on her far off gaze, I feel like she may have been talking more to herself rather than everyone else.

I was waiting for this moment, when the situation became so desperate for supplies that they would consider sending Lucie back out. I know that she would go in a heartbeat, especially if she knows it will help Bea, but I can't let her go out there when she becomes weak so easily making her vulnerable.

Having witnessed firsthand how bad it really is out there, especially in medical facilities, I can't in good conscience let her go out there in her current condition.

"I don't see a better option at this point. I mean we saw what she is capable of. I have faith that if she says she can do it that she can," Lochlan says, already having his mind made up ignoring everyone's concerns.

"Wait, did you already ask her?" I ask incredulous at

the thought he would do that without speaking to everyone first, assuming he was right to make that call on our behalves.

"No, but Chris, if she doesn't go we are not going to make it more than three months. Especially the sick ones. Without the proper equipment we are going to start losing lives. We need this far more than you can imagine," he pleads with everyone around the table, seeming to fight an uphill battle.

"What about having everyone get their own supplies?" I grasp at straws knowing this will never truly work, not with how large our community has become, but I try anyways.

"We can't have everyone going out to hunt for stuff, that would draw too much unwanted attention. It's just too dangerous. Especially with what Dr. Tanner is working on." Lochlan says exactly what I expected, but disappointment washes over me anyway, knowing I'm going to have to tell them about Lucie's condition and what I've discovered if I can't discourage their decision to send her out.

If betraying Lucie's trust is the only way to keep her safe, I'm willing to work everyday to earn it back to ensure that happens. I don't want to tell Lochlan what it is that makes Lucie different from Adira, but I will if I have no other choice. So fingers crossed I can play on the one thing I know will get Lochlan's attention, and that's making Lucie seem like a risk to everyone.

"Listen, Lochlan, you know of all people, I'm team Lucie. But right now, she's unpredictable, and you and I both know that that means dangerous. We don't know what could happen or what she really is capable of. We got a taste the other day in the field, but what if she turns that fight on our guys? She's a risk." I loathe myself as the words escape my lips, fighting the vomit that follows them. I can't believe I'm doing this to her, but if I can keep her safe, I will do whatever it takes.

Whatever it fucking takes.

"Do you really think Lucie's capable of something like that?" Lochlan asks, surprise in his voice at my declaration. Now I just need to drive my point home and make them see how wrong she is for this task.

"Ya, I do. I wouldn't want to be stuck out there with her in a confined truck when shit hits the fan," I lie through my fucking teeth, praying no one picks up the slight tremble in my voice.

"Chris, I don't think it's quite that ba—" Adira's words are drowned out by the sound of the front door slamming shut, causing all of us to whip our heads in that direction. I can see through the window as Lucie stomps across the compound towards the clinic.

Fuck!

CHAPTER 21

Lucie

I wake surrounded by Chris's scent, engulfed in his large bed, and I can't stop the smile that stretches across my face at the thought of what happened between us last night. I stretch out and feel the soreness of my body, the evidence of our activities, and with Chris of all people.

I blink my eyes open and roll over wanting to be closer to him, to feel his skin against mine, to confirm it wasn't some dream, but when I reach out the only thing I feel are cold sheets. Maybe he's in the kitchen or in the shower getting ready for duty today. I know he has a shift on the fence today, he told me last night as we lay in an exhausted heap of limbs.

I check the bathroom first, but nothing. I check the kitchen next, but the only thing I find is a mess of broken plates and dishes strewn across his linoleum floor. I quickly sweep it up before checking out back where he keeps his generator and things, but come up empty. He isn't here at all.

What the fuck?

Almost positive he must be at the station already, I quickly run home to shower and make him a coffee. That's right, I said coffee. No one knows I have a massive stash hidden in my place and I don't plan to share that information either. Perks of the job.

Or hazard pay, according to Bea.

I know for certain he hasn't had coffee in a very long time, since it would be me who gets it for him, and the fact we stayed up most of the night fooling around and talking, I'm pretty sure he's gonna need it today.

As I prepare the coffee in a to-go mug, also part of my looting, I can't help the giddy feeling of being able to give him something he needs and being the one who provides it for him, just like he's been doing for me. I'm sure we're gonna get a lot of looks and hear a lot of whispers at what's transpired, but we already talked about it last night, and neither of us gives a shit.

We choose us, no matter what.

Stepping through the front doors of the station, I can hear voices coming from the room where we met last time before I was bitten, and try to be as quiet as possible. I didn't realize they had a meeting, so I'll just sit here and wait until they finish then head back out to the shop to finish assessing the truck Chris's team demolished yesterday before I go sit with Bea.

I haven't been here for more than a minute when the sound of my name catches my attention. No one saw me come in, so I know they aren't talking *to* me, but about me. I inch my way down the corridor and stop a few feet down from the door, waiting to hear what prompted the use of my name.

Standing in the hall I can hear everything as they discuss the supply situation and the dire circumstances we're in, but when the mention of sending me out comes up, I can't help the excitement that builds at being able to go out on runs and contribute again.

I know I can get the supplies we need to get us caught back up and the equipment to help Bea and everyone else with the right team. Maybe Chris and a few other guys can come with me and we can do it together. I get lost in my own thoughts of mapping out how we could go about getting everything when their voices break through again.

"Do you really think Lucie's capable of something like that?" I hear Lochlan ask. Cleary, I've missed a crucial point in the conversation while plotting out my mission, but all that comes to a halt when I hear the next words leave the conference room from a voice I know all too well.

"Ya, I do. I wouldn't want to be stuck out there with her in a confined truck when shit hits the fan."

WHAT. THE. FUCK!

Chris's words affect me like a poison as his betrayal embeds itself in my system, overshadowing any other feeling I have towards him. *Had* towards him.

I guess now I know how he truly feels about me. I just heard it directly from his mouth. I thought after last night we had turned a corner, but apparently I was dead fucking wrong.

I hear Adira begin to speak, but I don't stick around to find out what else is said. Chris is in there making it sound like I'm some animal unable to control myself or my urges, when he was the one fucking pushing me every chance he got to get me to feed from him. As if he craved it too.

And then have the balls to say that? I'm so angry I'm actually physically vibrating.

After hearing Chris go to bat *against* me, I know there is no chance in hell that they're going to let me go on a run but I'm not about to ask for anyone's permission anymore.

If I can save Bea and countless others and not die, then I don't see another option. For months they've all tried to do what Bea and I did and for months, they failed. They all sit there, trying to find ways to get the supplies, but all they're doing is wasting precious time when I could already be out there.

Are they that stubborn that they don't want to admit that right now I'm their only hope?

Fuck what Chris and Lochlan or anyone else says. I'm going.

Knowing that I won't be able to rely on anyone here to aid me in my escape I'm going to have to be quick and smart about this. Starting with a distraction and organizing a crew.

Running straight to the house, I fly up the stairs almost tripping over my own feet as I power up my screen. There is only one person who can help me right now, so let's hope he's home. The moment the screen is up and running, I pull up the messenger service and send a quick text.

Lucie: *I need your help. Can you meet me in the city in 2 hours?*

Come on, come on, come on!

Rowan and his crew have helped us on many occasions to get in and out of the city unscathed, being our key ingredient to success on the clinic runs no one else is capable of completing. They create the distraction, Bea drives getaway and I'm the gopher gathering supplies for both crews. Bea and I leave their half of the supplies in a lock box a few blocks away from the hospital, payment for their services.

Finally, I see the three little dots pop up letting me know Rowan's is online and breathe a sigh of relief when his words materialize on the screen.

Rowan: *Of course. Whatever you need.*
Lucie: *I'm also gonna need a vehicle to transport medical equipment. And we're gonna need help.*
Rowan: *You got it. Where?*
Lucie: *The drop box.*

Standing in the alcove of the fence, furthest away from the gate and directly behind my tow truck I got stuck a couple of days ago when I saved Chris's ass, I wait for the perfect moment when I can climb through the small hole in the fence and make a bee line to my truck. If all goes as planned, I will have maybe five minutes tops to get it unstuck and take off before anyone makes it back to the gate. If I can get out undetected chances are no one will even notice the truck until it's already too late.

Any second now my distraction should take effect and I get ready to run. I pry the chainlink back ever so slowly and begin to squeeze through when the sound of gunfire permeates the air. That's my cue.

I take off towards my truck at a dead run, tossing the 2x4 chunk of wood under the rear tire to give it grip and hop in the passenger door, sliding across the seat and starting the truck in one fluid motion, praying to god this fucking works.

It roars to life instantly, and I hit the button to reel the hook back in and throw it in drive. I begin to rock the truck back and forth until the tire gets traction on the board, and the second I feel it stick I put my foot to floor.

Thank you Jesus.

I make sure not to kick up too much dirt and what not behind me to keep my escape as unannounced as possible and head towards the city.

After driving for about 15 minutes, I turn on the radio and tune into the compound station hoping to give myself a heads up the moment they realize I'm gone and give myself a chance to outrun them, but I lose range before that happens, making my drive into the city uneventful.

I relish in the quiet, knowing damn well it's not going to stay that way. I don't allow myself to think about last night and what it meant to me or what happened today. I refuse to acknowledge the betrayal I witnessed first hand from Chris, knowing that I can't afford to dwell on the what if's. If I focus on it too much I risk getting upset and prematurely draining my energy before we even get started.

Instead I remember the floor plan of the hospital and what's at stake if I fail. I remember what supplies I heard Dr. Tanner say she needed and create a mental checklist. Portable image machine, generators and lab processing machine with computer.

Get in, get out.

CHAPTER 22

Lucie

There's a heavy fog that blankets the city, creating an eerie atmosphere as I make my way through the downtown core to our meeting spot. I have a bad feeling in my gut but I push it aside and keep focused on my task at hand.

I pull into the parking lot and back my truck in, just in case I need to make a run for it and wait for Rowan and his team to show. I don't wait long before a U-Haul truck pulls up next to me, both the driver and the passenger's faces concealed by their large black hoods. I grip my bat a little tighter, ready just in case this isn't them and rest my hand on the ignition.

The driver hops out, rounding the front of the truck, and reaches up pulling back their hood, while simultaneously removing their bandana. Long black hair escapes the confines of the fabric, revealing a woman. A badass looking woman, but a woman nonetheless. And for some reason that puts me a little more at ease.

I step from my truck and meet her around the front of the vehicles, ready to get this mission started and over with before someone comes looking for me and/or we end up running for our lives.

"Where's Rowan?" I ask and wait for what feels like forever, while she looks me up and down before responding.

"That's me. Nice to finally meet you, Lucie," Rowan replies with an outstretched hand, but all I can do is stand there with my mouth on the floor, while I process the fact that this is Rowan. I'm not sure why but I just always assumed Rowan was a guy.

She chuckles at my stunned expression, not seeming offended and drops her hand, waving to her guys to come join us at the front of the vehicles to make a plan of action. Seven from her truck and three more pile out of a vehicle I hadn't even seen come in, and crowd around us.

"Everyone meet Lucie. Lucie meet everyone. We'll do proper introductions later, but for now, let's get this shit show on the road," Rowan announces as we all lean in over the floor plans to the hospital we are about to raid.

"We need equipment from three different locations at the hospital, so we're gonna have to split into three groups of four." I start off by showing them the locations on the map.

"We need a portable MRI machine, generators, and this lab machine in the picture and the computers to run it. They should be attached. We need to move large hauls quickly and quietly. Any suggestions?" I explain as everyone starts to divide into their groups of four.

"We can use blankets and bedding to keep the banging noises to a minimum," someone suggests, and we all make a mental note to stop and find bedding along our route.

Rowan and myself have the hardest task, along with two others, Jake and Travis I think they said their names were. We are going to get the MRI machine on the opposite end of the facility. Just because it's portable doesn't make it easy. It's very large and awkward to maneuver and since there's no elevators working, we're going to have to bring it around the outside to load it.

"I think we should leave someone at the truck. What if we need a quick getaway or someone to take out Z's while we bring the equipment and try to load the truck?" I suggest knowing that this is going to be our best option.

"But then one of the teams will be down a member?" someone points out, a little concerned that it could be their team short a person.

"Jake will stay with the truck," Rowan announces, and not one person disagrees, making her word final. She knows her crew better than anyone, and if she feels he is the one to stay behind, then so be it.

"Here's the plan. We are going to drop multiple coloured smoke bombs around the building and down the streets, hopefully drawing attention away from the truck and facility. Jake will stay with the truck and set up his sniper rifle on the roof," Rowan explains, now making perfect sense as to why she chose Jake to stay behind.

"Once we are inside the facility, we will all have fifteen minutes to procure our items and get back to the truck. If you do not make it in that time frame you will be left behind. The moment we leave here, it's radio silence until the mission is complete. Got it?" She asks, and a resounding sound of affirmation is heard from each person.

Smoke bombs are passed around and we split up into separate vehicles to deploy them in different directions.

Rowan jumps in the truck with me and we take off towards the hospital, her crew close behind.

"So where's Bea? She didn't want to do this one?" Rowan asks, trying to make small talk like we aren't on our way to do something akin to mission impossible.

"Actually, Bea is one of the reasons why I'm doing this run alone. She collapsed a few days ago and our doctor can't tell what's wrong with her without this equipment, and she isn't getting better." I fill her in on the comings and goings of Bea's condition.

"Shit! I'm sorry I had no idea. Don't worry, Luce, we'll get it all," Rowan says, completely confident in her crew's abilities.

Fuck, I hope she's right.

"So why haven't you been out on the city runs lately? I've seen Bea a few times, but each time she had a new partner. One of them was fine as fuck too. Dark hair, beard, tattoos...grrr," Rowan says with a growl at the end, and I can't help but burst out laughing. It's been a long damn time since I had a reason to laugh, but Rowan's relaxed tone and crude words, accompanied by that *Katy Perry* tiger roar just about kill me.

"What? He was," she says ,sounding offended, sticking out her bottom lip, while crossing her muscled arms, making me laugh even harder at the absurdity of it. I have to wipe the tears from my eyes before I manage to pull myself together as Rowan pretends to pout.

Her sullen attitude quickly dissipates as we pull up to our first marker and she reaches into her bag to prep the first bomb.

"Slow down up here." She points to a side street that runs parallel to the hospital.

After we release our smoke bombs, we pull around the back of the facility passing by Jake as he sets up on the roof of the U-Haul. I'm a little sad I'm gonna have to ditch this old tow truck, but it's worth the sacrifice.

"Travis is already inside and coming to let us in the back door where we are going to have to bring the machine out," Rowan informs me as I tuck the truck out of sight for anyone curious enough to leave the safety of their shelter and see movement.

"Let's do this." I fist pump Rowan before getting out and strapping ourselves in tactical gear and weapons, while waiting to be let in, but pause when I see she's looking at me strangely.

"You didn't bring anything to cover up?" her voice sounding surprised and a little concerned.

"No, it's fine. I'm good," I respond, trying to brush off her concerns without prompting too many questions.

"What do you mean it's fucking fine?" Rowan grinds out a little perturbed. I don't blame her as she is going into a suicide mission for someone she doesn't even know.

"I mean, it's fine because I'm immune." I shrug, trying to play off the fact that I may have or know of an antidote.

"Really? How is that possible?" Her voice raises in disbelief.

So much for not evoking more questions.

"Long story." Hoping that will throw her off at least until we can complete this run.

"Does it have anything to do with that bite mark on your arm?" She casually throws out making my head snap in her direction. She just smiles and nods to my now bare shoulder where my jacket was concealing the mark of death.

Fuck, I can't believe I didn't think to cover it up with a long sleeve or something before coming out here. And then I just wiped off my jacket without a second thought to gear up and never considering the consequences of others seeing it.

"Ya, it does. But listen, you don't have to worry, I don't want to bite you or anything."

"So...you're a half-breed?" she asks, seemingly curious and not put off by it one bit.

"It means, I can be bitten and not change. I have their strengths and one or two of their weaknesses," I say the only thing that I can possibly think of. I know it's from a movie, but that's all I got.

"Blade. Nice. So what, you're like a vampire?! 'Cause that's fucking cool. I want to be one too. Wait—if you bite me, will I turn?" Rowan asks excitement in her voice and I can't stop the chuckle at how she's taking the news I'm not human. Also, I have to appreciate the fact she caught my movie reference.

"No, I'm not a vampire. I'm not sure what I am anymore," I answer honestly.

"So are you dead then? Or undead I guess?" Her questions become over the top as more come to her.

"No, I didn't die. I just…changed," I deadpan.

"To what?"

Fuck, she's worse than a child with the fifty questions. Picture that cartoon kid always asking why, while wearing tactical gear, and a huge rifle.

"I don't know. Nobody does. I'm an anomaly," I say, my voice becoming soft at the fact that I'm still a question mark for everyone.

But I don't have time to dwell on my feelings, because in the next second, the door to the building gives a loud groan before popping open, exposing a smiling Travis.

"Coast is clear, ladies. The other groups are already in place."

And with that, all conversation ends and put our game faces on as we make our way into the building.

The halls are dark and littered with equipment and discarded items creating a sinister atmosphere that does nothing to chase away my earlier feeling of unease. The floors are stained, marked and scuffed with foot traffic, whether it's human or not is hard to tell.

"This way." Travis waves us forward, taking up the rear and keeping an eye out behind us.

We make it to where the large machine is abandoned and tucked up against the wall, covered in a sheet already, and making our job a tad easier. We wrangle it away from its stationary position and begin to push it, but the second we do a god awful screech is echoed down the silent halls of the now abandoned building and we freeze. None of us speaks or even breathes waiting to see if our clatter garnered unwanted attention. After several minutes of us being statues, we regroup and keep going.

But the moment we push it again the same sound permeates the air.

"Fuck, we are never going to get that thing back to the truck unnoticed. Not like that," Travis quips. Thanks captain obvious.

Luckily, this is not my first trip and I always come prepared knowing how this new world works. I pull a small squirt bottle from my pocket and poor it over the wheels of the cart to loosen and grease them up.

"Well look at you, hybrid, stepping up and showing us how it's done," Rowan jokes, eliciting a confused expression from Travis. I don't acknowledge his look or the comment from Rowan as we wiggle the wheels to ensure I've silenced them.

"Nicely done. Now let's get the fuck outta here." Rowan's take charge attitude is back, and I don't fight her for control. She is the one helping me and it's her crew, so what she says goes.

We manage to get the machine to the truck without any other hiccups, as well as all the other teams. I've never been more thankful than I am at this moment knowing that they all came through to help Bea.

We don't waste any time as we all help load, keeping the noise down as much as possible. It's hard with metal equipment on a metal truck and metal ramps. Some sound is to be expected.

However, the sound that we hear is not that of metal or the equipment we are currently trying to liberate from the facility. I stop, unsure that I heard correctly and take a step away from they crew as they grapple the last of our haul into the truck.

Another howl breaks the silence and we all freeze and this time I'm sure. That howl is not from a fucking dog.

Fuck! That's the sound of a Demon Z. And based on the fact that the sound was closer this time means it's closing in on us. The problem is, where there's one, there's always more.

"MOVE IT!" I barely have time to get the words out, when three of the scariest, loudest Demon Z's come around the corner at a concerning speed, their screech deafening.

"What about you?!" Travis shouts as Jake takes his last shot before having to get in and drive.

"GO! I'll distract them." I grab the handgun and two machetes that were set aside by someone and head towards where the infected are coming at us firing off a shot at the closest one.

"Lucie, NO!" Rowan shouts.

"Meet me around front when you're done loading up. I will draw their attention away, but when I come running, make sure you're ready to go!" I shout out, before taking off at a dead run away from the vehicle and changing the trajectory of the incoming z's.

Here we go again.

Having done this before and being aware of my strengths and what I'm capable of now, I feel like a total badass knowing that I'm practically invincible. Ya, I can still die, but it sure is a helluva lot harder to kill me know. And I relish that feeling and own the shit out of it.

I hear shouts from behind me, but I can't afford to look back, sensing the Z's swallowing the distance between us.

I make it around the corner and launch myself onto the roof of a discarded car and hold my ground here. The high pitch squeal of the Z's sound out, bouncing off the brick buildings of the city scape and amplifying it by a hundred.

I cover my ears as the shrill cry wreaks havoc on my sensitive hearing, almost buckling my knees in the process. I push through the pain as the Z's close in on me, circling the car for a moment before the first one launches up.

I don't waver as I spin on my heel, deftly removing the head and watching as it plunks down into the mass of claws and teeth.

Black ichor coats the blade and everything it touches as I begin the process of removing limbs and heads of anything that moves in my vicinity. But the herd becomes too large and more and more infected join the chaos that is literally surrounding me.

Out of nowhere, shots begin to ping off the vehicles surrounding me, thinning the herd and giving me an opening. I don't know who it is, and frankly I don't give a shit.

I leap from the roof of the car and take off towards where I told Rowan to meet me, but the second I round the corner I see the U-Haul idling and zombies litter the area around it.

I start to shoot at whatever I can, but my aim is not great. One of the many reasons I use my bat or blades over firearms. Not to mention, bats and blades don't run out of ammo.

When the group surrounding the truck realize I'm shooting from behind they turn and face me ready to get their meal on the go. I fire off what's left of the bullets in the gun I confiscated and make my way to the truck.

I'm gonna have to fight them all off, but I have no other option. I have to get this equipment back before it's too late.

CHAPTER 23

CHRIS

"I'm going after her!" I shout at the room as they all gather around the table trying to figure out what to do next. I'll tell you what we need to do, we need to go after Lucie before she gets herself killed.

"Don't be stupid, Chris, you won't make it back alive and you know it. You barely made it with Bea!" Lochlan fires back, irritation in his voice. But his words only piss me off further.

"Don't fucking tell me what to do, Lochlan. You and I both know that if the situation was reversed and Adira was out there, you would have already been gone, so don't preach your holier than thou bullshit to me."

"Chris," Lochlan sighs, exasperation evident in his voice as he runs his hand through his beard. "If you go out there, you could potentially make things worse. The best thing we can do right now is wait until we hear something from her. Think of Lucie," he finishes off, but that was not the right statement to make right now.

"I AM FUCKING THINKING ABOUT LUCIE! Why

do you think we're even here right now?!" I scream at him and get right in his face ready to go toe to toe with him.

I'm ready to walk through hell, and take on the devil himself in order to bring Lucie home safe right now, and I almost dare someone to get in my way at this point.

"Chris, listen to me. How do you think Lucie would feel if she returned and you were gone? You and I both know that it would destroy her if something bad happened to you."

Fuck! He's right.

I storm out of the station, fuming mad at the leash Lochlan's put on me, telling me to stay put while Lucie is out there all by her damn self. Even though I understand it, doesn't mean it doesn't piss me the fuck off.

Somehow, ending up back at the clinic, I barge through the doors and into Bea's room, throwing myself down in the chair beside her.

"What's wrong, Romeo? Your girl kick your ass for being a moron?" she chuckles, thinking she's clever.

"She left," I say, my head in my hands as helplessness consumes me.

"What? Who?" she asks, clearly confused about the happenings being cooped up in here.

"Lucie! She fucking left to go do the medical run everyone else is trying desperately to complete by her damn self." I stand, sending my chair skidding across the floor as I begin to pace.

"She's stronger than you think, boy. She's been through a hell of a lot worse than this and come out on the other side. Trust me, she'll make it," Bea says, her words sure and clear, but I'm not convinced.

Why does everyone keep saying that?!

No one knows if she will make it back or not, for Christ's sake. No one even knows which location she's going to or when the fuck she left.

Thoughts of what could possibly happen to her begin to flourish and dread threads its way in, weaving its poison into my mind and taking root. My heart rate skyrockets and my chest tightens, taking me to my knees as my body begins to shut down. Tears cloud my vision and overwhelming despair is all that I can process as I wrap my arms around myself, desperately trying to hold it together but failing.

Brittle fingers grip my upper arms as I'm being shaken, but I can't make out who it is.

"Christopher!" Bea's voice finally breaking through, but sounding so distant. I reach for the sound and clawing my way out from the hole I'm in but I can't gain ground and I just continue to slip further into nothingness.

"Boy, you had better get your ass up. I did not drag you in from the snow that day only to have you leave her when she needs you the most. You promised me that you would take care of her when I couldn't and I am going to hold you to that until the day you die."

Bea's angry voice breaks through just a bit more, but when she cuffs me upside the head, I'm able to latch onto that pain and drag myself through the darkness towards her words.

"Now get your ass up, get out to the fence, and wait

for our girl to come home. 'Cause she is coming home. You hear me?!"

Bea's conviction is the only thing that breaches my consciousness enough to pull me out of my purgatory and see reason.

Bea was the one who hauled my ass to the hospital the day Lucie was bit because she believed I would be the one to care for her when no one else could and she couldn't be more right.

I pull myself together and prepare myself to sit at that fence and wait until she returns, even if I'm waiting forever.

She'll make it.

CHAPTER 24

Lucie

I step into the swarm and commence hacking at whatever reaches towards me. Head, hands, arms and whatever else I come in contact with are removed from its body as I push my way to the truck.

Black and red liquid drips down my blades and hands, making it hard to hold on as I wield them through the frenzy of bodies as hunger drives them forward. I'm starting to slow down as my limbs become like weights, making it almost impossible to lift them and I stumble slightly.

I hear in the distance the horn blaring from the truck, not sure if it's to catch my attention or of those infected around me, but that's all it takes to catch me off guard and I'm thrown to the ground with extreme force.

I scramble around trying to get my feet under me and get out from whatever crashed into me but it's no use, the weight is too great. I'm at the bottom of a dog pile as teeth and claws try desperately to breach my leathers as I continue to fight off whatever I can.

I hear a door shut, followed by shots as zombies rain

down around me. I hear the sound of Rowan shouting to get the fuck up, but before I can pull myself up, I feel that familiar searing pain as teeth puncture my flesh.

"FUCK!" I scream into the air as a new wave of adrenaline crashes through me and I renew my attack on the infected around me.

I swing out and a head lolls off and tumbles away, I use the lifeless body to block the others coming in for a bite and continue to hack my way through from the inside while Rowan and whomever else cuts down the mass from the outside.

"Start the truck!" I yell as I kip to my feet and begin to feel the telltale sign of power coursing through me.

"Run, Lucie!" Rowan shouts again, but I don't need to run now. I can feel my body begin to adapt to the pain and my strength increases in spite of the venom.

"START THE FUCKING TRUCK!" I shout again as I leap up using a fallen zombie body as a launch pad and throw both arms out to my side and removing multiple heads as I part my way through the herd of z's.

I land hard on bended knee, but don't pause and catapult myself towards the truck. I yank open the door and fold myself in slamming it shut behind me as the zombies throw themselves at the doors and windows.

"GO, GO, GO, GO!" I slam my hand on the dashboard hoping to spur Rowan into gear and it works. Her foot slams on the gas, tossing us back into our seats as she pries the truck away from the undead and leaving a trail of hungry z's in our wake.

She takes a corner a little too fast, sending me into the

door and I groan from the pain as the rush of endorphins slows, magnifying the agony and making my vision blink.

"Shit, Lucie, you were fucking bit!" Rowan says while trying to keep her eyes on the road.

"It's fine. Just keep going." I brush it off, needing to keep focused on staying conscious and not on the unbearable .

I can feel my body begin to shut down from the bite, as venom courses through my body, urging the hunger into high gear. The need to feed is pressing down on me and if I don't do it soon, I'm not exactly sure what that will mean for me.

Or anyone else.

CHAPTER 25

CHRIS

It's been hours, but I'm not leaving this gate entrance until Lucie is back inside these walls, where I know she's safe and alive. If I have to wait forever I will, because without her, I have no life to go back to.

"Hey man, how you holdin' up?" Tripp asks, coming to sit next to me on the watchtower. Truth be told, I really don't know how I'm holding up to even try to answer, so I just shrug. Everything in my shitty existence is disappearing and there's nothing I can do to stop it.

"She'll be back, Chris. If anyone can make this run, it's fucking Lucie. Have some faith," he says while resting a reassuring hand on my shoulder.

That's the thing, everyone thinks I don't think she's capable of the run, but I know better than most that she is no doubt the most qualified to do that run. They don't realize what the run could mean for Lucie. They don't understand what has been going on with her and what we've recently discovered. Lucie is in more danger than they could even fathom right now.

Granted, she could drink anyone's blood and still have

the same effects, but we discussed that we wouldn't let anyone know about this until we knew what this meant because everyone might not take too kindly to the fact she is drinking blood to survive.

The sound of an approaching vehicle snares my attention and I'm instantly on my feet, grabbing the binoculars to see better. I hear Tripp radio into Lochlan to let him know about an incoming vehicle, but I don't listen further.

Come on, little one, please be you. Please be you.

When the truck comes into view I strain through the binoculars praying for a glimpse of blonde hair or her black bandana, anything that will prove it's Lucie, but that's not what I see at all.

"That's not Lucie!" I shout out, pressing the alarm on the walkie talkie alerting everyone of the incoming unknown.

In seconds, everyone moves into position, rifles at the ready, prepared for whatever is coming in hot.

Shit, why the fuck aren't they slowing down?

"They aren't slowing down. Get ready!" Lochlan booms over the channel.

Fuck!

Before we have the chance to brace ourselves, the truck crashes through the gates, pulling the front panels and everything down with it, causing a lot of ruckus. They plow through cars, and tear down the streets heading straight for the fucking hospital.

Shit.

I see Tripp as he stops to set up his shot to take out a rear tire of the U-Haul, hoping to not send it flipping into the buildings or people as the rest of us ready ourselves to chase it down.

When the rear passenger tire blows we all hold our breath, but when it does nothing to slow the trucks momentum. Along with Lochlan, Tripp and Grey, we all take off at a dead run towards the vehicle, hoping at least one of us will be able to catch it or take it out before it's too late.

Out of the corner of my eye, I see Adira come from between the buildings running full tilt for the truck. Her speed is something to marvel as she catches the speeding truck and hops on the drivers side door smashing in the side window.

"Adira, stop!" Lochlan's shouts can be heard from every corner of the compound as he chases the vehicle carrying his girl and leaving a path of destruction.

"Someone stop that fucking truck!" Lochlan roars over the radio as it begins to weave out of control.

Suddenly, a body is tossed from the drivers side door and the trucks brake lights come on as it slows down to a stop just outside the hospital.

As soon as it's stopped, Adira jumps out, grabbing something from the back. Wait, not something, *someone*, and runs into the clinic. The discarded figure begins to lumber to their feet, a little worse for wear and heads in the same direction.

Shit, Bea!

I pick up my pace.

"Stop them!" Lochlan shouts, but all of us are too far away to get there before they make it inside.

Fuck, I hope they're not infected.

Lochlan, Tripp, and I fly into the hospital searching for whoever came in here and see a dark haired woman dart into a room at the end of the hallway.

"Stop!" we shout in unison, but it's too late, she's already inside with whomever else is in there.

Thank fuck it's not Bea's room.

We make it to the room ready to restrain this woman and toss her in a cell, but we all come to a stop when we see her standing next to Lucie, bloody and bruised but alive. The woman stands there holding Lucie's hand while she writhes in pain, whispering words of encouragement in her ear and pushing damp strands of hair away from her face.

"Where the fuck did Adira go?" Lochlan's thunderous voice vibrates the walls, causing the woman to start and Lucie to wince.

"Who the fuck are you?" I demand of the person holding my woman's hand as I make my way further into the room. Tripp begins to circle in behind her at the same time as I keep her attention forward on me.

"Who the fuck are you?" she sasses back. This chick has balls, and based on the muscle she's packin', she actually might.

"Don't take another step mountain man or you're gonna have a new haircut, catch my drift?" she tosses over her shoulder at Tripp, more aware of his presence than she let on. I see Tripp freeze and curse under his breath, drawing a feminine chuckle from the woman.

"Last time I'm gonna ask. Who. Are. You?" I emphasize the words, making sure she understands this is not a fucking game.

But before she can answer, Lucie's eyes snap open donning the most vibrant yellow glow I've ever seen, and a keening cry let loose into the air causes my body to crumble at the sound.

Fuck, she needs to feed.

Dr. Tanner comes crashing through the doors with Adira hot on her tail ready to jump in if needed.

I know that nothing they do will work fast enough, but I step back and let them flit about her. But I already know. Her body is violently pumping the virus through her veins from the bites but unlike Adira, her body is accepting it and demanding more instead of shutting down and fighting it off.

Watching her thrash around in pain does something inside me, and I don't hesitate as I step up to the opposite side of the bed and begin rolling up my sleeves. The dark haired woman doesn't say a word as she watches in fascination, while Dr. Tanner and the other's continue to try and work out what's happening.

I know what's happening and what she needs, and it's nothing they have or can do here.

I go to pull my switchblade from my pocket, but it's not there. I look up ready to ask one of the guys, when the raven haired Rambo pulls one from her tactical vest, causing a chain reaction of shouts and weapons being drawn.

She tosses her hands in the air and steps back with a wide smirk on her face as she nods at me to continue, clearly privy to our little secret. I whip it open and drag the blade across the opposite palm I used the first time we did this little dance.

I know she's gonna be pissed at me when she finds out that I did this in front of everyone, but if it's gonna save her life, then too fucking bad. She can be mad at me her whole fucking life, as long as she's alive, I don't give a shit.

"What the fuck are you doing, Chris?" Tripp asks, his eyes locked on my hand as I step closer to Lucie's bed, settling beside her and pulling her to my chest.

"She's different." And that's all I say as I bring my hand up and hover it over Lucie's mouth.

"What the fuck are you doing, Chris?!" multiple shouts and gasps sound from every corner of the room as a small scuffle breaks out. I see Grey fighting to restrain Lochlan, but it's all background because all my attention is on Lucie.

Come on, baby, wake up.

Drip.

"Chris…"

Drip.

Come. On.

"Chris…" someone tries again, but I ignore everyone except the woman in my arms as I keep my hand over her mouth, letting the blood slide down her throat.

"Come on, little one. I need you to drink it, baby. Come on," I coo in her ear as I gently rock her body back and forth, praying to anyone that will listen to send her back to me.

"Come on, Lucie. I need you to *drink*," I try again, but still nothing, her body completely unresponsive and her breathing so shallow it's hard to tell if she's even doing it anymore.

"Chris I think—" but someone stops Adira mid-sentence, as the room watches on in silence as I shatter, begging for Lucie to come back to me. Pleading for her to open her eyes.

"Please, Lucie, I need you," I whisper as a tear rolls down my cheek and onto hers.

Lucie's eyes suddenly snap open as she reaches up and latches onto my hand, and I almost sob in relief as I feel the first pull from her lips. She sinks her teeth in but I don't flinch this time at the feeling of arousal that ignites inside me. This time I embrace it. But all too soon her lips pull away and her head lulls back, completely uncon-scious again.

Gasps and various "What the fuck?" are heard and echo around the room at what has transpired, but I don't care. Nothing will ruin the fact that Lucie is alive, in my arms and mine. Nothing.

CHAPTER 26

Lucie

F<i>uck, not this shit again.</i> I think to myself. That same damn incessant beeping is back, but at least it's a steady rhythm and not that obnoxious tone from last time.

However, unlike last time, when I try to open my eyes they actually cooperate and I'm forced to squint against the overhead lights that seem to rival the sun. I go to lift my hand to cover my face when I'm met with resistance.

Now what?

I lift my head, with effort and am met with more bodies than I was expecting. Rowan sits on a loveseat with a sleeping Tripp handcuffed to her wrist while she reads whatever book she was able to scrounge up.

Chris sleeps on the hospital bed with me, his head on my thigh using me as a pillow, with one hand in mine and the other wrapped under my legs. I smile and reach my other hand down and run it through his hair, basking in his affection, no matter how short lived.

A throat clears and I turn my head to find Bea sitting beside my bed in a wheelchair, all wrapped up in blankets looking paler than when I left.

"Hey, girl," she croaks, her voice thick with emotion as she takes in the sight of me.

"Hey," is all I manage before she hauls her ass out of that chair faster than I could fathom considering her condition, and she wraps her arms around my neck. I pull her into the bed with me and Chris, not caring if I jarr him awake or not and wrap my arms around her, as every emotion for the past three months drowns me.

"Shhh, it's ok, girl, I got you," she soothes, rocking me as a mother would a child, and I cling to her even tighter, refusing to let go ever again.

"Hey, punk?" she says into my hair.

"Ya?"

"Mind lettin' up a bit? My fragile bones can't take all the superhero strength." I let up and pull back as I hear chuckles covered by coughs come from where Rowan sits.

"Damn, girl, you missed one hell of a show," Rowan says from her seat and lifts her new bracelet to emphasize, and shaking Tripp awake in the process. He grunts when he realizes it's just her moving around but sits upright immediately when he sees I'm awake.

"Hey, Luce, how you feelin?" Tripp asks.

"Surprisingly, I feel pretty good," I say truthfully. I'm not in pain like I was the last time I ended up in this predicament.

"You gave us quite the scare," he says as his eyes pass by mine and land on Chris, who is no longer sleeping, just watching the exchange between myself and everyone else.

"Who wants coffee?" Bea asks from her chair, and I shoot a death glare at her conveying with my eyes that it had better not be part of my stash she's offering to everyone.

"You have fucking coffee?!" Rowan's voice similar to that of a child on Christmas morning, full of wonder and magic.

"Oh, sweetie, you would be shocked what w—" Bea's words are cut off and all conversation halts at the arrival of Dr. Tanner.

"Hey, Lucie, I'm glad you're awake. How are you feeling?" she asks walking into the room and taking in the group around me.

"I feel pretty good, thanks."

"No need to thank me, I did nothing. It's you I should be thanking, and Rowan, of course," Dr. Tanner replies, elation evident in her voice while gesturing to Rowan and myself.

"You hear that mountain man, thanks to me." Rowan points out sarcastically while emphasizing herself.

"Yes, I could not thank either of you enough. This could potentially be a new beginning for everyone. That being said, Bea, we are all set up and ready for you now," Dr. T says, stepping towards where Bea, now back in her chair, is sitting.

"Awe, we were just going to go get coffee," Rowan says as Dr. T begins to wheel Bea out.

"You get nothing but a one way trip back to the police station, now that we know Lucie is awake and can talk for herself." Tripp cuts off Bea while trying to manhandle Rowan out of the chair. Rowan just smiles at me and winks as Tripp pushes her through the door.

"I like it rough, soldier, so your little tactic to push me around does nothing but turn me on."

I can't hear Tripp's reply from the hallway as he continues to push her out the door, but I snicker at her comments, knowing damn well that he is gonna have his hands full with that one. I kinda hope she sticks around after all this.

The second everyone is out of the room, Chris crawls up the bed, kneeling beside me, and pressing his forehead to mine. His hands come up and frame my face as he breathes me in and I watch as a single tear falls from his eye, landing on the sheets beside me.

"I almost lost you," he whispers against my lips, his voice so broken it slices my insides at how vulnerable he is right now and I don't have the heart to push him away.

His mouth fuses to mine, but he doesn't take it further or push for more, he just holds me there as though he needs this reassurance.

A moment of clarity seeps through my muddled brain and I press my hands to his chest, pushing back ever so slightly, remembering the events leading up to this moment and the feelings of betrayal return.

"Wait! Don't pull away." Chris's words barely a whisper, cause me to pause.

I don't know why I stop, maybe I'm a glutton for punishment or maybe it's the fact that after the shit that went down out there today the thought of his betrayal isn't as harsh, but either way I stop.

"I'm sorry, Lucie. For everything. For yelling, for what I said, for how I treated you. *Been* treating you. I'm so fucking sorry. I just... Please don't pull away from me."

The sound of his apology breaks through the last of my willpower to be mad at him and I crash my lips to his, taking everything he has to give. I grip his hair and tug, absorbing the growl he emits at my actions.

He pulls back to look in my eyes while slowly climbing off the bed. He moves to shut and lock the door, closing the blinds on his return trip and tossing aside his shirt at the same time.

Chris stands at the end of the bed removing his pants and boots in a quick striptease before climbing back on to do the same to me. Luckily the gown makes it super easy for him and he makes quick work of it.

The second it's off he crawls across my body and holds himself above while staring into my face. "Don't ever leave without me again. I can't do it anymore." His tone leaving no room for argument.

I hold his stare and for the first time I don't fight him on this topic. If he wants to come on the runs with me then so be it, but I won't stop doing them.

"Ditto."

With that our mouths collide, both tongues demanding entry as we battle for dominance. I get the upper hand and flip him onto his back, straddling his waist, surprised at my own strength all things considered. I hold his gaze as I lean forward and rest my opening against his tip, but he wants no part of it and slams me down onto his hips in one fluid motion.

I cry out at the invasion, but the slight pain mixed with

the pleasure of having him inside me causes me to grind down harder, seeking friction against my clit. Chris's hands slide up my thighs and he digs his fingers in, sure to leave bruises, still trying to gain control from the bottom by keeping me still and thrusting upwards.

Not this time.

I place my hands on his chest and lean forward slightly, taking the weight off my legs and redistributing it onto my palms as I hold Chris down, taking what I want. With each lift of my hips he slides almost all the way out until I slam back down onto him and forcing a growl from his throat.

"Fuck, little one, you're not even gonna give me a fighting chance," he grits his teeth as I continue my movements and gathering speed, getting closer to the edge with each pass on his shaft.

I don't think Chris realizes that when I say my senses are heightened, I mean all of them, because if he thinks he's going to come before me, he's wrong.

"Come on, little one..."

Goosebumps break out over my skin at his words and the moment Chris pushes his hand between us, making contact with my clit, I fall. Hard.

My breathing becomes ragged, my moans become a crescendo of pleasure as my orgasm slams into me, my eyes now a vibrant yellow. I feel the hunger begin its trek through my system, but it doesn't feel as overwhelming like it usually does, instead it's more of a dull manageable ache.

"Do it." His taunt loud in my ear, his hand coming up

between us. Except this time I don't think twice before I take what I crave from him. It's no longer just a need, but a deep rooted craving that I don't want to get from anyone else.

He reveals a small cut on the side of his wrist, and the moment my lips touch his skin, his movements become erratic and after three more pumps, he comes. His entire essence swims within me, blending with my own and creating a strength I've never known.

The feeling of him beneath me shatters every fantasy I've ever conjured, because this by far is the sexiest thing I've ever seen. Chris throws his head back into the pillow, lips parted in a silent moan, veins stretching up the column of his throat as the look of euphoria replaces the concentration that was there only moments ago. His hands come up and grip both sides of my hips, coaxing me forward and back over his length at the pace he needs to finish, and I go willingly.

I crash down to the bed beside him as we both try to catch our breaths, and he tucks me into his side, nuzzling where my neck meets my shoulder. His fingers run circles over my skin, making it tingle in every spot he touches.

"I know I have a lot to apologize for, Luce, and I am sorry. And I will spend every single day apologizing to you, for the rest of our existence, if you'll let me?"

I'm not exactly sure what his promise entails, but I intend to find out.

EPILOGUE

TRIPP

I sit across from her cell and catalogue her every curve and feature from her head to her toes. Long black hair, shaved on both sides. Not in a harsh way, but still feminine. Dark brown eyes, framed with long dark lashes and flawless sun-kissed skin. She's fit, muscled, an alpha female to the core. And what I wouldn't give to fight her for that dominance.

My cock rises to attention at just the thought of having to pin her down and make her submit to me.

Fight me, kitty kat.

"Let's try this again shall we? How did you two meet?" I ask for what has to be the millionth fucking time. Why she won't make things easier on herself, I have no fucking clue, but she is stubborn to the core this one.

"Ask, Lucie," she replies dryly.

"So, the two of you got all that equipment by yourselves?" Her jaw ticks at my words and I can see real emotion peek through that rough exterior she fools most with. But not me. I can see she is a vulnerable girl wanting to be taken care of for once not the other way around. To have someone take that control from her and let her breathe, if even for a moment.

"Ask, Lucie," she repeats.

She doesn't look away or cower under my stare, her fierceness never failing. The only thing giving away her agitation is the tick in her jaw at each question I throw at her.

"I can do this all day, so why not make it easier on yourself and just answer the damn questions." I try to reason with her, but can see by the look on her face that I won't get a fucking straight answer no matter what I ask.

"Better make yourself comfortable," I grind out as I stand to leave, hearing her growl at my back.

That's fine, kitty kat, roar all you want, but I'm gonna be the one to make you purr.

ACKNOWLEDGMENTS

First and foremost, I have to thank you for reading this book. This is now my second book ever and the elation I feel is indescribable. I can't wait for you to read Rowan and Tripp's story, because let's be honest, it's going to be hot as fuck! Thank you for following me on this incredible journey and supporting me and I can't wait to see where it goes from here.

I need to thank Reyne Morris Clark for always pushing me like the slave driver she is, but I'm ok with that because without her, this wouldn't be possible. Thanks girl for being with me this whole ride so far.

An enormous thank you to Dee Garcia who makes all my words look beautiful with her graphics and covers and formatting. She puts up with my never ending questions, my stalker tendencies, unorganized ass and is pretty much at God status in my world. I know that sounds creepy, and I don't care. You have done so much for me and I will literally thank you in every single book for the rest of my life, for just existing and being you. Thank you lady, I love you! xo

I need to thank my husband for putting up with my moody ass and bringing me food and liquids throughout the whole process and fueling my passion. I love you Mike.

To my family, if you're reading this, don't you dare judge me. I fucking warned you!

ALSO BY N.M. BLACK

The Pandorum Series

PANDORUM (BOOK ONE)

DARK HORIZON (BOOK TWO)

ROWAN'S STORY *COMING SOON* (BOOK THREE)

The Swiss Series

HER *COMING SOON*

ABOUT THE AUTHOR

N.M. Black is a writer and a lover of all things dark, living in Ontario, Canada where she also works as a medical secretary. Living on caffeine, sarcasm and movie quotes, N.M. spends most of her downtime either reading, writing, or binge watching Harry Potter, Friends and anything Marvel. Looking to take the Indie scene by storm, her author journey has only just begun.